P9-CLQ-045

FAVORITE TALES FROM GRIMM

Illustrated by Mercer Mayer

text retold by Nancy Garden

FOUR WINDS PRESS NEW YORK

LIBRARY OF CONGRESS CATALOGING IN PUBLICATION DATA

Kinder- und Hausmärchen. English. Selections.
Favorite tales from Grimm.

Translation of selected tales from: Kinder- und Hausmärchen.

Contents: Little Snow White—Rumpelstiltskin—The two brothers—[etc.]

1. Fairy tales—Germany. [1. Fairy tales. 2. Folklore—Germany] I. Mayer, Mercer, 1943– . II. Grimm, Jacob, 1785–1863. III. Grimm, Wilhelm, 1786–1859. IV. Title.

PZ8.K572 1982 398.2'1'0943 82-70410
ISBN 0-590-07791-0 AACR2

PUBLISHED BY FOUR WINDS PRESS
A DIVISION OF SCHOLASTIC INC., NEW YORK, N.Y.
COPYRIGHT © 1982 BY MERCER MAYER
ALL RIGHTS RESERVED
PRINTED IN THE UNITED STATES OF AMERICA
LIBRARY OF CONGRESS CATALOG CARD NUMBER: 82-70410.
1 2 3 4 5 86 85 84 83 82

To Arden and Goldie Holbrook

LITTLE SNOW WHITE

ONE snowy winter day, a beautiful queen sat at her window sewing and watching the snow. Her palace was so splendid that its walls were made of marble and its doors and window frames of darkest ebony. As the queen sat there, she admired the way the cool winter light made the ebony window frame look smooth as black satin, and while she was thinking how lovely it was, she pricked her finger carelessly with her needle. When she shook her hand, a few drops of blood fell outside, where they glistened, making a vivid red pattern against the pure white of the snow on the windowsill. "I wish I had a little daughter," the queen sighed, "who had skin as white as snow, lips as red as blood, and hair as black as ebony."

Not long after that day, the queen gave birth to a baby girl. But alas, the new mother lived only long enough to see that her wish had come true. Her child did have skin as white as snow, lips as red as blood, and hair as black as ebony.

The king mourned the death of his wife for a year or more, but then out of loneliness he married again. The new queen was beautiful, but in a cold, cruel way and, unknown to the king, she, although not quite a witch, knew evil magic. This new queen was so vain that she could not bear the idea that any other woman might be more beautiful than she, and so she used her magic to fashion a mirror that would always tell her who was fairest in the land. Every morning the queen stood in front of her magic mirror and said:

Looking glass upon my wall,
Who is the fairest one of all?

So far the mirror had always answered:

O Queen, 'tis you who are fairest of all.

At that, the queen always smiled and went through the rest of the day confident that no one was more beautiful than she.

But as Little Snow White, which is what the first queen had named her child, grew, she became more lovely every day. Hers was a soft, gentle beauty, not harsh like the new queen's. And one day, when Snow White had reached the age halfway between a child and a woman, the queen looked into her mirror and said:

Looking glass upon my wall,
Who is the fairest one of all?

and the mirror answered:

O Queen, you are fairest of all in this place,
But Little Snow White is fairer of face.

For a moment the queen was stunned, and thought she had not heard correctly. So she asked the mirror again, and again came the reply:

O Queen, you are fairest of all in this place,
But Little Snow White is fairer of face.

At that, the queen flew into a rage and threw her hairbrush across the room in anger. From that day on, whenever she saw Snow White, she could barely contain her jealousy. Soon she hated Snow White so much that she could not sleep and could barely eat. At last she called one of the king's huntsmen and ordered him to carry Snow White off into the forest and kill her. "Make sure you obey," she said, when the man grew pale. "Bring me back her liver as proof that you have done the deed."

The huntsman nodded, but the word "yes" stuck in his throat, and all the way into the forest with Snow White he wondered what he would do. At last he drew his knife, but Snow White, seeing what was what, began to cry and said, "Oh, huntsman, please spare me! I will run away deep into the forest and never show myself to the queen again. Only spare my life!"

The huntsman gladly agreed, and sheathed his knife. On the way back to the palace he killed a fierce wild boar, and brought its liver to the wicked queen, who ate it. "Now," she said to herself with great satisfaction, "I can be at peace at last."

In the meantime, Snow White, alone in the forest, found it a less friendly place than she had imagined, and was terribly frightened. She had no idea how to find food, or where to sleep, or how to keep herself safe from wild beasts. The wild beasts, however, had no interest in her other than to look at her with pity as they passed.

Snow White could think of nothing to do but walk, so walk she did, and when she was so weary she thought she could not go another step she came to a little cottage—truly a little cottage, for everything about it was so small it could almost have been built for a child.

Snow White knocked at the door, but since there was no answer and no one seemed home she pushed it gently open and went inside.

There, clustered around a cozy fireplace, were seven small, stuffed chairs, and on a table nearby were seven books and a pipe rack holding seven little pipes and a jar of fragrant tobacco. In the corner was a neatly set table, with seven little chairs pulled up to it, and at each of the seven places there was a plate and a knife, fork, and spoon, and a bowl and a mug. On the plates were meat and peas and in the bowls were soup and in the mugs was wine. Snow White was so hungry and thirsty that she had a little soup from each bowl—it was barely warm—and a little bite of cold meat and two or three peas from each plate, and a tiny sip of wine from each mug—for she did not want to deprive the rightful owners of their meal.

Then she found the bedroom, and in it were seven little beds, each of which she tried in turn, for she was very tired. The first one was too long, the next one too short; the third was too wide and the fourth too narrow; the fifth was too hard and the sixth was too soft—but the seventh was perfect and so, sighing contentedly, Snow White lay down and fell fast asleep.

Soon the owners of the house returned. They were seven dwarfs, each slightly smaller than the next, who made their living mining for gold in the mountains. As soon as they lit the candles, they could tell someone had been in their house, for though nothing was gone and nothing harmed, things had been rumpled or moved ever so slightly.

The first and largest dwarf said, "Someone has been sitting in my chair!"

The second and next largest dwarf said, "Look—my pipe has fallen off the rack!"

The third said, "Who can have been eating my soup?"

The fourth said, "And my peas—surely I had more!"

The fifth lifted his mug and said, "And my wine!"

The sixth said, "And my meat!"

And then the seventh said, "The bedroom door is open—someone must be in there!"

So they went into the bedroom, and each one noticed that his blanket was wrinkled or his sheets creased or his pillow not quite at its usual angle, and they each said, "Someone has been lying in my bed!" But then the seventh with a great cry said, "Someone is *still* lying in mine!" and they all rushed over and found Snow White, sound asleep.

"Oh, my, oh, my," said the dwarfs one after the other. "What a beautiful little girl—poor child, she must have been lost in the forest. Let us tiptoe out so that she can sleep."

So the seven dwarfs went back to their dining table and ate their meal—which by now was quite cold indeed—and talked of this and that, but mostly of Snow White and how she might have gotten lost. And when the time came for them to go to bed, she was still asleep, so the seventh dwarf slept one hour with each of his brothers so that she would not have to move.

In the morning, Little Snow White woke up and saw the dwarfs all around her and was so frightened that she cried out. But then they woke up and asked her what her name was and where she was from and how she had come into the forest. When she told them, they took great pity on her and invited her to stay with them.

"How kind you are," said Snow White, "for it is true that I cannot go home. But surely there is something I can do for you in return."

"Indeed there is," said the largest dwarf. "Perhaps you noticed that our soup was cold last night when you sampled it."

"Yes," said Snow White, "and I am sorry I had some of your soup, but I was so very hungry. . . ."

"No, no," said the second dwarf, "do not apologize. You needed the soup more than we."

"What my brother meant," said the third dwarf, "was that because we are away all day in the gold mine, we must set out our own dinner before we leave."

"For we are too tired when we come home to do it then," put in the fourth dwarf.

"And so," said the fifth, "it is always cold by the time we come home."

"But if you could cook for us . . ." began the sixth.

". . . we could have a hot meal," finished the seventh—and they all looked at her hopefully.

Snow White laughed in delight—for the dwarfs were really quite charming—and said, "Of course I will cook for you! And clean your house and," she added, looking at their clothes and noticing a hole here and a button off there, "do your mending as well."

"Hurrah!" the dwarfs shouted in chorus—and so it was settled.

Snow White had much to learn about cooking and cleaning and sewing, for as a king's daughter she had always had servants. But the dwarfs helped her, and she soon learned. Every morning they went off to the mine, and she cleaned and sewed for a few hours and then had plenty of time to read or think or gather flowers till she had to cook dinner. "But do not go far from the cottage," the dwarfs warned her every morning, "and go inside if anyone comes."

"And do not let anyone in," said the largest dwarf, "ever, ever, ever—for the wicked queen your stepmother will find out soon enough that you are still alive."

The dwarfs were right, for in a few days the queen longed to hear her looking glass tell her she was once again the fairest, and she went to it and said:

Looking glass upon my wall,
Who is the fairest one of all?

and the mirror answered:

O Queen, you are fairest of all in this place,
But seven dwarfs live in the forest so deep,
And Little Snow White their household does keep—
And she, O Queen, is still fairer of face.

And the queen was so angry she threw her scent bottles across the room and would have punished the huntsman gravely for not carrying out her orders had he not prudently left the kingdom.

"I must think of a plan," the queen said to herself, "for Snow White cannot be allowed to live."

The queen went to her dressing table and with her powders and paints she transformed her face into that of an old woman, and then she went to the rag bag, and found in it clothes even the servants had thrown away, and she dressed herself like a peddler-woman. Taking a basket from the kitchen, she set out for the forest.

When she reached the seven dwarfs' cottage, she knocked on the door and said:

Ribbons and laces,
Sashes and pins—
Come, pretty lady,
Come—let me in.

Snow White went to the window and called out, "Hello, peddler-woman, what are you selling?" She was pleased and excited, for she had never been allowed to speak to peddlers when she lived in the palace.

"Oh, I sell many things," said the wicked queen, "but the prettiest are these lovely sashes." She held up several, some made of brightly colored silk and some of wool, and Snow White could not resist them. There can be no harm, she thought, in letting that nice old woman in, and so she opened the door to her.

"Tch, tch, tch," clucked the wicked queen when she was inside, "someone should take you in hand, child, and teach you how to dress. Here—let me just put this pretty sash around you and you will see what a difference it will make—there!" And as the wicked queen put the sash around Snow White's waist, she pulled it so tight that Snow White could not catch her breath, and she fell down as if dead.

"How fleeting your beauty is," said the wicked queen gleefully, looking down at Snow White, whose lips were now quite pale. "It will be of no further trouble to me!" And she left with light steps and a light heart.

That evening when the dwarfs came home, it was a sad sight that met their eyes, for the door of the cottage stood wide open and Snow White lay motionless upon the floor. They knelt by her and chafed her wrists and cheeks, but she did not move and she did not answer when they called her name. Then they lifted her up.

"Look!" cried the seventh and smallest dwarf. "Look—she has never worn that sash before!"

"Someone must have come here and given it to her," said the sixth dwarf.

"The queen!" cried the next dwarf.

Quickly the dwarfs untied the sash—and almost as soon as they did, Snow White moved a little and began slowly to breathe in and out. And when she came to life again and told them about the peddler-woman, they said, "Snow White, that was your stepmother, the wicked queen! We tried to warn you before—*please* do not let anyone in while we are gone!"

Snow White hung her head and promised that she would not.

That same night when the wicked queen got home, she went to her mirror and said:

Looking glass upon my wall,
Who is the fairest one of all?

and the mirror answered:

O Queen, you are fairest of all in this place,
But seven dwarfs live in the forest so deep,
And Little Snow White their house still does keep—
And she, O Queen, is still fairer of face.

When the queen heard that, she was so angry that she threw her powders and paints across the room, and became red in the face with rage. For a few days she was so angry she could do nothing, but when her anger turned to cold fury she set about forming a new plan. "I shall make a beautiful comb," she said to herself one morning, "a comb so beautiful no young girl could resist it, and I will put poison on it, so that when it scratches her—and it will be sharp—she will fall down dead."

The wicked queen made the comb, and poisoned it, and then with what was left of her paints and powders she made herself look like an old gentlewoman who had fallen on bad times, and she went again to the dwarfs' cottage. "Oh, mistress," she cried piteously when she had knocked and Snow White had come to the window, "I am a poor widow and have so little I must now sell all my precious trinkets in order to buy bread for my poor children. Would you not like to buy this pretty comb? It was given me at my wedding."

Snow White was so tenderhearted that she could not resist this plea and she reached out of the window for the comb.

"Oh, do let me in, kind mistress," said the wicked queen, keeping back the comb, "and I will show you how to fasten it."

"I am not allowed to let anyone in," said Snow White, "but I will lean out the window to you."

And so she did, and the wicked queen put the comb into her hair, twisting it so roughly that it scratched Snow White's scalp. As before, Snow White fell down as if dead, and the wicked queen, laughing evilly, went back to her palace.

It was not long before the seven dwarfs came home and saw Snow White lying on the floor as if dead. They tried to revive her as before, but nothing did any good until the largest of the dwarfs said, "Look—she never wore this comb before," and the second dwarf said, "Someone must have come here and given it to her," and the next dwarf cried, "The wicked queen!" and plucked it out.

As soon as the poisoned comb was removed from her hair, Snow White began to stir slightly. When she was at last better, the dwarfs scolded her for letting someone in. But then she told them what had really happened and they said, "But Snow White, you must not go near *any* stranger who comes, no matter how pitiful. Your stepmother will do anything to destroy you; you must be constantly watchful."

And so Snow White promised again to be careful and to guard against all strangers.

That night when the wicked queen got home, she went to her mirror and said:

Looking glass upon my wall,
Who is the fairest one of all?

and the mirror answered:

O Queen, you are fairest of all in this place,
But seven dwarfs live in the forest so deep,
And Little Snow White still their household does keep—
And she, O Queen, is *still* fairer of face!

The queen in her rage threw a chair across the room, and it broke into many pieces. This time she was so angry that without delay she made a poisoned apple, taking care to make it as perfect as she could, and so pretty that no one could resist it. She put the poison in one side of the apple only, and on the side that was not poisoned, she painted the tiniest of bruises. When the apple was finished she disguised herself as a farmer's wife and went back to the dwarfs' cottage.

This time when she knocked upon the door, Snow White did not come to the window but instead stood against the farthest wall and called out, "Please go away, whoever you are. I am not allowed to go near strangers."

"That does not matter to me," the wicked queen answered. "There has already been such demand for my apples that I have only one left. I will simply rest here and eat it myself." And she sat down on a stone and took a tiny bite out of the side of the apple that had the bruise in it.

This made Snow White curious, so she went to the window stealthily and looked out. And there she saw a harmless-looking farm woman, sitting in front of the cottage nibbling the most beautiful apple she had ever seen. Oh, it was so beautiful that it made her mouth water just to look at it!

"What a lovely apple that is," Snow White called—for surely there would be no harm in speaking to the woman from a distance.

"It is indeed," said the wicked queen. "It is the best of the lot, and they were all the finest we have ever grown, my husband and I." She smiled engagingly at Snow White. "I have saved the best one for myself, it seems," she said, "but you are looking at it so longingly, I will be happy to give you half."

Now what harm, Snow White thought, and what danger, could there possibly be in that—for the woman has already eaten some of the apple herself.

"Would you?" she called out eagerly. "Oh, that would be so kind!"

And so the wicked queen cut the apple in half, and through the window handed Snow White the half that had no blemish.

Snow White thanked her and put the fruit to her lips, taking a bite. And no sooner had she done so than she fell down once more, but this time she was cold as ice.

"Nothing can save you now, my beauty," chortled the queen, "for I have used my strongest poison this time, and since you have swallowed it, you will never rise again. So, Skin-White-as-Snow, Lips-Red-as-Blood, Hair-Black-as-Ebony, what good is your beauty to you now? This time no one will ever be able to wake you up again."

And the queen went home to her mirror and said:

Looking glass upon my wall,
Who is the fairest one of all?

and it answered:

O Queen, 'tis you who are fairest of all.

The queen was so overjoyed that she danced around the room, knocking over a table as she did so.

That evening when the dwarfs came home they found Snow White lying on the floor, and though they chafed her hands and cheeks, and loosened her sash, and looked for combs in her hair and anything new upon her, they found nothing and they could not make her live. And so they wept, and set about making a coffin.

"We will make one of glass," the largest dwarf said, "and we will trim it with gold from the mine, for our lovely Snow White is too beautiful to bury deep in the dark ground."

So they made a beautiful glass coffin, richly trimmed, and they wrote "SNOW WHITE—A PRINCESS" on it in gold letters, and they put the coffin in the prettiest part of the woods, right out in the open. They took turns guarding it day and night, and birds and forest animals often came and guarded it with them.

Years went by, and winter and summer Snow White lay in her coffin and, though she never stirred, she looked as beautiful as she had in life. Her skin was still as white as snow, her lips as red as blood, and her hair as black as ebony.

One day a prince came into the forest, and he saw the coffin and marveled at Snow White's beauty. The smallest dwarf, who was guarding it at the time, told him her story. "What a terrible thing," said the prince. "She looks as gentle and good as she is lovely."

"Oh, yes," said the dwarf, "that she was," and he told the prince how Snow White had kept house for them, and how it had been her kindness that had allowed her to be victim of the poisoned apple.

"I cannot bear to part with her," said the prince, gazing at the coffin. "I will give you all my gold for the coffin, and I will carry it home to my father's palace where Snow White will be able to lie in state forever."

"We cannot part with her," said the smallest dwarf, and the next smallest, who had just arrived for his turn as guard, agreed. "We will not let you take her away for all the riches in the world," he said.

"Then perhaps you will give her to me," said the prince, "for I feel I will die if I cannot always see her. I will cherish her as if she were my wife," he said, "and I will never marry."

The dwarfs were moved by this and could not refuse him, so they called their brothers and at last they all decided to give the prince the coffin out of pity, for he looked at Snow White so tenderly.

The prince then ordered his servants to pick the coffin up, and as they carried it away, one and then another of them stumbled on tree roots, jarring the coffin badly. And that sent the piece of poisoned apple out of Snow White's throat, where it had lodged—and, as she had not swallowed it after all, she opened her eyes and in all ways came to life again.

"Where am I?" she asked, lifting the lid of the coffin and looking around.

"You are in the forest with me," said the prince joyfully, and told her who he was.

"And with us," said the dwarfs, who had stayed to see her safely away. "Oh, dearest Snow White!" And they helped the prince lift her out of the coffin and stand her upon her feet, and they all hugged her and danced around her for joy.

"Snow White," said the prince, when the rejoicing had subsided, "I fell in love with your beauty when I saw you lying in the coffin; then I fell in love with your kindness when the dwarfs told me of it; and now, seeing you alive, I have fallen in love with you yourself. Will you come with me to my father's palace and be my wife?"

"I will," said Snow White, "if I may visit my friends the dwarfs and if they may visit me, whenever any of us likes."

"Of course," said the prince. "You may have anything you want that I can give you, always."

"Then I will come with you," said Snow White and, after saying good-bye to the faithful dwarfs—but only until the wedding, which they would attend—she left with the prince.

Now one of the wedding guests, because she was a queen, was Snow White's stepmother, but she was not told in advance who the bride was, because of her anger and her temper. While she was dressing for the wedding, she brushed her hair in front of her mirror and said:

Looking glass upon my wall,
Who is the fairest one of all?

and the mirror answered:

O Queen, you are fairest of all in this place,
But young Queen Snow White is fairer of face.

And at this the wicked queen was so angry she ripped the mirror from the wall and threw it across her room, shattering it into a thousand pieces. One of the pieces hit against the ebony window frame, and flew back and pierced the wicked queen's heart, and she fell down dead, never to harm Snow White or anyone else again.

RUMPELSTILTSKIN

A POOR but boastful miller had a beautiful daughter. Every place he went he bragged about his child, saying she was more beautiful than the sun and the moon, that her voice was like an angel's, that she was wiser than the king's advisers, and that she could bake, sew, spin, and weave better than anyone else in the world. Now one day the miller went to the palace to deliver some flour and, as the king's cook was busy, he was taken to see the king himself. As usual, he fell to talking about his daughter, but he talked even more than usual this time, for he knew an opportunity when he saw one and hoped that the king might take her to wife. "She is more beautiful than the sun and the moon, your majesty," he said, "and her voice is like an angel's." On he went, listing the girl's beauties and talents—but the king had heard many a hopeful father speak thus of his child, and yawned with boredom. At last the miller, in desperation, said, "And, your majesty, I have saved the best for last. Not only can my child bake, sew, spin, and weave better than anyone else in the world—but she can also spin straw into gold."

Now the king, despite his wealth, was a greedy man, and at this he stopped yawning, leaned forward, and said, "Ha—hum—what is that you said, miller?"

"I said, your majesty, that my daughter can spin straw into gold."

"Well, well, well," said the king. "I have heard many a father praise many a daughter in much the way you have praised yours, but never have I heard of a girl who could spin straw into gold. Bring her to me and we will see if you are telling the truth."

So the miller went home, and told his daughter she must go the next day to the king's palace, but he did not tell her what he had said she could do. "When the king sees her beauty," he told himself, "that will be enough for him." And he went to sleep well content, and the next day took his child to the palace and left her there.

That evening the king took the miller's daughter into a large room full of straw, sat her down at a spinning wheel, handed her a reel, and showed her others nearby in a pile. Then he said, "Now, my dear, let us see if you can do what your father says you can do."

"What is that?" asked the girl, puzzled and frightened at the same time.

"Why," said the king, "he says you can spin straw into gold. You will have all night to do it. I will come at dawn and if you have not spun every bit of straw into gold, you will be sorely punished." The king then left, locking the door behind him, and the poor girl looked around at the straw in despair and began to weep—for she had not the slightest idea how to begin. She tried once or twice to treat the straw as if it were flax or wool, but it was so stiff it broke apart in her hands.

At last, when she was weeping bitterly, the locked door opened and shut so quickly it was almost as if it had not moved at all, and an ugly little man appeared. "My, my, my," said the little man, "I thought I heard someone weeping and now I see it is true. And what might the trouble be, mistress?"

"Oh, sir," said the girl, "my father has made an idle boast to the king that I can spin straw into gold—but, alas, I know not how to do it. The king will come at dawn and if I have not done it, he will punish me. What am I to do?"

The little man came closer and picked up a bit of straw, twirling it between his thumb and forefinger. "Not bad straw," he remarked. "I daresay I could manage the job. What," he asked, putting his face up close to the girl's, "will you give me if I do it for you?"

"I have very little," said the girl, "but I do have this necklace."

"Hmmm," said the little man, "not very good, but I daresay it will do." He reached for it, and then told the girl to get up from the wheel. He sat down at it himself and instructed her to keep handing him straw as he spun. In a trice he had filled the first reel and picked up another, and in a trice that one was full also, and so on, until all the straw was gone and in its place was reel after reel of spun gold.

At dawn the little man vanished. When the king arrived soon thereafter, he saw the reels of gold and his face broke into smiles, for he had been sure the miller was lying. He let the girl sleep and spoke gently to her when she woke—but the next evening, because he was so very greedy, he showed her to an even larger room full of straw and again told her to spin it all into gold by dawn or be severely punished. "Do this," he said sternly, "if you prize your life."

The girl sat down at the wheel, and tried to do as the little man had done the night before, but, alas, the straw remained straw no matter how she held it. And so again she began to weep.

Suddenly the door opened and shut again as before, and the little man appeared. "What, again?" he said. "I see you have learned nothing!"

"Oh, sir," said the girl, "I tried to do what you did but could not. And now the king says that if I prize my life I must spin all this straw into gold by morning."

"Well, well," said the little man, "I see I must come to your aid again. What will you give me this time?"

"I have even less now than I did before," said the girl, "but you may have this ring if you like."

"Hmm, hmm," said the little man, examining it, "not much of a ring, but I daresay it will do." And again he seated himself at the wheel and again filled reel after reel with spun gold.

The next morning when the king came he was pleased at what he found, but his greedy heart still cried out for more. So after the girl had slept, he took her into another room, the largest yet, and again told her to spin all the straw there into gold by morning. "And if you succeed," he told her, "I will make you my queen." He said this not out of any great love for her—although he was beginning to feel as fond of her as a greedy man could—but because he knew that if he had a wife who could spin straw into gold he would always be rich, no matter what happened to his kingdom.

Once again the girl tried to do what the little man had done, but could not, and once again he came to her and asked what she would give him if he did it for her. "Alas, " she said, "I have nothing left."

That was the opportunity the little man had been waiting for. "The king will make you his queen if the straw is turned to gold, will he not?" he asked.

"Yes," said the girl. "At least that is what he said."

"Well, then," said the little man, "I will take your firstborn child in return."

And so the girl agreed, saying to herself that even if the king did marry her, she might never have a child.

By morning the room was full of neatly piled reels of gold and the king smiled when he saw them and ordered his servants to prepare for a wedding, and to invite the old miller who had bragged so about his child. The wedding was held in all splendor, for of course the king now had unlimited gold with which to purchase dainties to eat and fine clothes to wear and to hire musicians to play wonderful airs and dances in every corner of the palace.

By the time the young queen gave birth to her first child, she had forgotten all about the promise she had made to the little man, for she had not seen him since. But he came to her nonetheless, while her baby was asleep in its cradle, and said, "I have come for your child, miller's daughter."

The young queen's heart fell, but she said bravely, "Begone, little man! I am queen now; you cannot give me orders."

"Oh, can't I?" said the little man nastily, and he blinked and turned the queen's favorite gold necklace into rope.

Then the queen saw that he had power over her, and wept. "Oh, sir," she said, "I will give you anything you want, only do not take my child!"

"Well, dear me," said the little man, feeling a stab of pity for her, despite his hard heart, "I will give you three days' grace. If in three days you have not guessed my name, then I will take your child. I shall come tomorrow and see what name you think is mine."

The queen spent that whole night sitting at a table in her room, writing all the names she could think of upon long sheets of paper. And the next day the little man came to her and said, "Well, what is my name?"

"John," she said.

"No," said he.

"Jonathan," she said.

"No," said he.

Then she said, "Abel, Abraham, Alexander, Alexis," and he said no to all. So she said, "Balthazar, Bradford, Bruce, Brian," and he said no, and on she went through the alphabet, saying every name she knew, and to all he said no, and left her, calling over his shoulder, "Two more days!"

That very same day the queen sent messengers all over the kingdom, each with a scribe to write down every name he heard. And after they all returned she spent the whole night crossing off their lists the names she had already mentioned, and adding a few new ones, not on the lists, that she had thought of during the day.

When the little man came back to her, she said, "Is your name Adonis?"

"No," he answered.

"Is it Bellerophin?"

"No."

"Is it Boythorn or Caradoc?"

"No and no," he said.

"Dumbiedikes or Elmo or Fradubio?" she asked, and went on through her entire list, but each time the little man shouted "No!" more gleefully than the time before.

"One more day!" he cried as he left. "And then the child is mine."

The queen hugged her baby to her breast and wept, but then she ordered her messengers out again, telling them to listen in all unlikely places. She told her most trusted messenger to try to follow the little man and also to find out if anyone knew him and his name. And all that night the queen sat at her window, thinking and thinking of what name she could possibly have missed. Toward dawn she went into the king's library and scanned his books and manuscripts for new names, but she found only a few she had not already guessed.

Early in the morning the messengers came back, and each one handed her a list of a few new names. And then finally the special messenger returned, running, and he fell to his knees before the queen in exhaustion and said, "Oh, your majesty, I was about to give up, for no one knew the little man or had seen him, when I came through the forest to the tall mountain that is on its other side. And there cut into the rocks was a little door and in front of the little door was a cooking fire, and in front of the cooking fire was an ugly little man much as the one you have described. He was singing and dancing and this is what he sang:

Baking day has come and gone,
And brewing day arrives tomorrow.
The queen's child then will be my pawn,
While the queen is lost in sorrow.

Straw into gold is nothing to me,
And neither is a guessing game—
I know the queen will never see
That Rumpelstiltskin is my name!

At that the queen cried out in joy and thanked the messenger and rewarded him handsomely. And then she kissed her baby and they both slept peacefully until the little man came to her again.

When he arrived, there was a look of great smugness on his face. "Well," he said, his hand on the cradle, "let us get it over. Have you guessed my name, I wonder?"

"Perhaps," said the queen, putting on a mournful expression. "Is it Sallust?"

"No," said the little man.

"Is it Schwanthaler?"

"No."

"Is it Tranjan? Or Underwood? Or Villemain?"

"No, no, no!"

"Well, perhaps it is Waksman? Or Xerxes? Or Yamashita? Or—perhaps—Zorn?"

"No, no, no, no!" said the little man, jumping up and down impatiently. "You have finished the alphabet many times over. The child is mine."

"I forgot one," said the queen quickly. "Just one more, back a bit."

"One," said the little man, reaching for the baby, "but only one."

"Is your name," said the queen, "by any surprising chance—Rumpelstiltskin?"

The little man stared at her, his mouth open in amazement. Then his face turned quite red and he shouted, "You learned that from the Devil! From the Devil!"

"No," said the queen, picking up her baby, "I learned it from you yourself, for you sang it as my messenger went by:

'Baking day has come and gone. . . .' "

And at that the little man was so furious that he stamped one foot and then the other right through the palace floor and the ground beneath, and disappeared forever.

THE TWO BROTHERS

In a far land many years ago there lived two brothers. One was a goldsmith and very rich, but evil. The other was a broom-maker, and as good as his brother was evil, though his only riches were his twin boys. The twins were handsome children and exactly alike; the only difference was that one was a single hour older than the other.

One autumn day, when the leaves on the trees were turning gold and scarlet, the broom-maker went into the forest to gather twigs for his brooms. While he was there he spotted a bright gleam among the leaves and, first thinking that it was only a patch of autumn color, he ignored it. But then he heard a merry chirping, and looked closer, and saw that what he had mistaken for golden leaves was instead a beautiful golden bird. Thinking that the bird would fetch him enough money to feed his family for a long time to come, he threw a stone at it, but the stone only grazed the bird's wing, and one golden feather floated down. "Well," said the poor broom-maker, "I will take it to my brother nonetheless; since he is a goldsmith, he will know if it is worth anything."

The evil brother examined the feather carefully and said, "Yes, it is gold, pure gold at that," and he paid his brother for it.

The next day the broom-maker was again in the forest when the same bird flew off a nest high in a tree. When the broom-maker climbed up and looked in the nest, he found what appeared to be a golden egg. He took the egg to his brother also, and again his brother said, "Yes, this is of pure gold," and paid him for it. "But you know," said the goldsmith craftily, "I would pay even more for the bird itself."

The next day the broom-maker returned to the forest, this time with the purpose of capturing the golden bird. After searching for a few hours he saw it perched on a branch, and this time he was able to bring it down with a stone. Happily, he took it to his brother, who paid him well for it.

Ah, but although the goldsmith had paid well for the bird, the bird itself had special qualities that only the goldsmith knew of, and was of far more value than the money he had given up for it. For the goldsmith had known all along that whoever ate the heart and liver of a golden bird would find a gold piece every morning under his pillow, and it did not trouble him to keep that knowledge from his own brother. It did not trouble him either to keep it from his own wife. To her he said that he wished her to roast the bird for his dinner. "Roast all of it," he said, "and prepare something else for yourself, for I will eat it all. I especially want the heart and the liver," he said, "so take care that nothing ill befalls them."

The wife did as her husband said, and left the bird roasting on a spit over an open fire in her kitchen while she went outside to fetch water. And at this moment in came the broom-maker's twin boys and saw the spit turning and the bird becoming a delicious golden brown.

"Mmm, that looks good," said the boy who was older by an hour.

"It does indeed," said the younger boy.

And at that moment, as they watched, two small pieces of meat fell out of the bird onto a pan below.

"No one would know," said the older twin, "if we ate those two small pieces."

"No one would even miss them," said the younger twin.

And so the two boys each reached for a morsel of meat and each popped one into his mouth.

Just then the goldsmith's wife came back, lugging two heavy pails of water, and saw her nephews chewing. "What are you eating?" she cried.

"Oh, Aunt," they said, "just two small bits of meat that fell out of the bird. We thought it would not matter."

"Begone," said the wife, shooing the boys away, and she took the bird and peered inside. "Alas, it is as I thought," she said. "They have eaten the heart and the liver!" So she killed a chicken, and roasted its heart and liver and then just before the golden bird was done, put them inside. "Here you are," she said, carrying the platter to her husband, and he ate the whole bird, but ate the heart and liver with special relish.

But the next morning when he felt under his pillow, there was nothing there.

It was not like that with the twins, for that same morning, when they got up, a piece of gold rolled out from under the older one's pillow— and then, when the younger looked under his pillow as well, there was a piece of gold there, too. "Father, Father!" they cried, running to the broom-maker, "just see what we have found! Did you put these under our pillows?"

"Not I," said their father. "Where would I get gold pieces? I have put away the ones your uncle paid me for the golden bird, to save and spend only as we need them." He smiled. "Some good fairy must have rewarded you for a good deed," he said, patting his sons' heads.

But the next morning there were two more gold pieces, and the next and the next. Finally the broom-maker became alarmed and went to his brother for advice.

The goldsmith, who had spent his days in anger at his wife for replacing the true heart and liver with false ones, was now more angry still, and he could not bear the thought that his brother might benefit from the gold his sons were bringing him. "It is the work of the Devil," he said to the broom-maker. "You must send your sons away, for they are in the Devil's power, and you will be ruined if you let them stay."

The broom-maker had heard many stories of how the Devil had taken men's souls and he feared that above all else. So, with tears in his eyes, he took his twin boys, blindfolded, deep into the forest, waited till they had fallen asleep from weariness, and then, weeping, left them.

When the two boys awoke, they tried desperately to find their way home again. But in a while a huntsman came by and asked them who they were. "We are lost," they told him, "and our father has left us because every morning we each find a piece of gold under our pillows. He is afraid that it is the work of the Devil and that evil will come from it."

"Evil from money," said the huntsman, "is all a matter of how one uses the money, not of the money itself. But if your father fears the Devil so deeply, he will only turn you out again if you return to him. Come—I will take you home with me. I have neither wife nor child and would be proud to be father to two fine boys like you." And so he took the twins home and raised them as his own, and every morning he took the two new gold pieces and put them away in a bag for when the boys were older. And every day also he took them into the forest and taught them the craft of hunting. "For," he said, "when you are grown, even though you have gold, something may happen to it and you will have to earn your living. Besides, it is not good to be idle, no matter how rich you are."

The boys were good pupils and by the time they were grown, the huntsman was pleased with their progress. On their eighteenth birthday, he said, "Today we will see how much you have learned. You will each have a trial shot, and if you handle it well, you will be ready to be huntsmen on your own."

In time a flock of geese flew overhead in a triangle, and the huntsman said to the older twin, "Shoot one down from each corner." The boy did as he was told perfectly, and the huntsman embraced him and said, "I could not have done better myself." Then another flock came by, flying in the shape of the figure three, and the huntsman told the second twin to shoot down one from each of the three's points. The second twin accomplished his test as perfectly as his brother, and so they all went home to have a fine meal in celebration.

But as they sat down to eat, the older twin said, "Father, we have a request, and we will not eat till you have granted it."

"And what is that?" asked the huntsman.

"We wish to prove ourselves *by* ourselves," said the younger twin. "You have cared for us kindly, sheltered us warmly, and taught us thoroughly, but we do not feel we can truly call ourselves huntsmen till we have traveled alone and seen how we get on."

"Well spoken, my boys," cried the huntsman, clapping them both on the back. "Bravely spoken! Of course you shall go, with my blessing."

And then they all three ate and drank with gusto.

The next morning, the boys set off, each with a pouch full of food and a brand-new gun given him by his foster-father, and as many of his gold pieces as he wanted to take. When the twins left, the huntsman held out a bright, shiny knife, saying, "Take this with you also, and if ever you separate, plunge it into a tree at the place where you take leave of each other. Place it so that one side of the blade faces where one of you has gone and the other faces where the other has gone. If one of you returns to that place, he will be able to see how his brother is, for if the side of the knife facing in the absent one's direction is clean, all is well with him—but if it is rusted, he is dead."

So the brothers took the knife, and embraced their foster-father once more, and left, walking over hills and across valleys till they at last came to a forest that was so vast there seemed no end to it. The food in their pouches soon ran low, and the younger twin said, "We will have to put ourselves to the test now, brother, for we shall soon starve if we do not find food." And so they loaded their guns, and began looking for game.

Soon a hare ran by and they lifted their guns to their shoulders, but the hare said:

> Please do not shoot, oh, huntsmen bold!
> For as you see, I am too old.
> Spare me, and nothing will you rue:
> Two younger hares will follow you.

The two brothers dropped their guns in surprise and the hare ran into the underbrush and soon returned with two little hares, who scampered around so charmingly that the huntsmen could not bear to shoot them. And so they walked on, and the two little hares followed them, hopping along behind.

In a while one of the brothers spotted something moving along the path ahead, and as it was a fox, both raised their guns again, but the fox turned and cried:

Please do not shoot, oh, huntsmen bold!
For as you see, I am too old.
Spare me and nothing will you rue:
Two younger foxes will follow you.

And sure enough, as soon as the huntsmen lowered their guns, two playful, young foxes leapt onto the path, jumping over each other so merrily that both huntsmen laughed and could not think of shooting them, either.

"But we must find something soon," said one, "for we have very little food left."

In a while a wolf walked stiffly out of the thicket beside them, but when they raised their guns to shoot, he cried:

Please do not shoot, oh, huntsmen bold!
For as you see, I am too old.
Spare me, and nothing will you rue:
Two younger wolves will follow you.

And the wolf was as good as his word. Two strong, young wolves soon joined the foxes at their play and followed along behind, and the huntsmen marveled that the young hares showed no fear, nor did the foxes or the wolves bother them in any way.

The afternoon sun had passed its noontime peak and was beginning its long afternoon descent when a bear bumbled out of a cave beside the path, and again the huntsmen raised their guns. But the bear said:

Please do not shoot, oh, huntsmen bold!
For as you see, I am too old.
Spare me, and nothing will you rue:
Two younger bears will follow you.

And there appeared two merry, young bears, nearly grown, who cavorted so pleasingly that the huntsmen laughed and let them follow also.

"This is all very well," said one, munching on the last crust of bread, "but the next beast we see, we must shoot."

But the next beast was a noble lion, who shook his mane and said:

Please do not shoot, oh, huntsmen bold!
For as you see, I am too old.
Spare me and nothing will you rue:
Two younger lions will follow you.

And it all fell out as before, with two strong and youthful lions joining the procession.

And now the sun dipped toward the horizon, and both brothers were growing irritable with hunger, so one of them turned to the foxes and said, "Foxes always know what is what, and where chickens roost; tell us, are there any farms nearby where we might find some food?"

"Oh, yes, master," said one of the foxes, "not far from here there is a village—just follow us." And the foxes ran ahead and the brothers and all their other animals followed behind. The foxes led them out of the forest and into a village, where there was food for all.

And so for a time the two brothers traveled around with their animals behind them, but though they were always able to find food, they were not able to find work, for two huntsmen was one too many for anyone to hire at once. So at last they decided to separate. Each one took a hare, a fox, a wolf, a bear, and a lion, plus his own gun and food pouch, and together they plunged the knife their foster-father had given them into a tree at the place where they took their leave of each other. Then the older one went to the east, and the younger one to the west.

In two days' time, the younger brother arrived in a strange-looking town—strange because every house was hung with black crepe, as if the whole town were in mourning. The younger brother went straight to the inn where he asked for lodging for himself and his animals, and the good

innkeeper provided the animals with an empty stable and the huntsman with a fine room. And when the hare had found himself a cabbage, and the fox a hen, and the wolf, bear, and lion had eaten also, thc huntsman looked to his own comfort. When he was settled, he said to the innkeeper, "Is the town in mourning for some great personage? All around I see nothing but black crepe and sad faces."

"We are all sad indeed," answered the innkeeper, "for tomorrow the king's only daughter must die."

"Is she very ill, then?" asked the huntsman sympathetically.

"No, she is very well," said the innkeeper. "But on the hill that rises above our town there lives a fearsome dragon with seven fire-breathing heads, and every year he must have a maiden to eat or perish. And now there are no maidens left in the town save the king's daughter, so tomorrow she must be taken to the hill, and must climb up it and let the dragon eat her."

The huntsman shuddered and said, "But why does no one kill it?"

"Alas, sir," said the innkeeper, "many have tried—brave knights and valiant soldiers—but all have lost their lives to the terrible beast. There is nothing to do," he finished sadly, "but give the dragon his due—although the king has promised that whatever man will slay the beast may have his daughter's hand in marriage and will become king after his death. But it is too late for that, for tomorrow will soon be here."

"What a great pity," the huntsman said thoughtfully—but he said no more, and went to bed.

The next morning, however, he took his animals to the hill, and bravely climbed it. There at the top was a chapel, so the huntsman went inside and found on the altar three cups full of liquid. Under them was a sign that said: "He who drinks these cups dry will be stronger than all others, and only he who is stronger than all others will be able to use the sword that is under the threshold. With that sword, he will be invincible."

The huntsman was a cautious fellow, so he went out without drinking of the cups, and dug under the threshold for the sword, which indeed was there, heavy and sharp and brightly shining. He reached down to grasp it and pick it up, but found he could not move it, so he went back inside, drank the cups dry, and went out again to the sword. This time he lifted it easily and brandished it above his head.

While the huntsman was practicing with the sword at the top of the hill, watched by his faithful animals, a sad procession made its mournful way to its foot: the maiden who was to be sacrificed; her father, the king; his marshal; and many courtiers, all weeping. As she approached the hill, the poor maiden saw the huntsman and thought he was the dragon. She wept, though up until then she had been bravely silent. "Princess," said the marshal, "you know what will befall the village if you refuse: The dragon will destroy us all, and will not leave a house or a stable or a barn or even your father's palace standing. You must go."

And so the brave maiden left off weeping, embraced her father, and went up the hill. The king turned back toward the palace, followed by his courtiers, for he could not bear to watch, but the marshal remained.

When the maiden got to the top of the hill, it was not the dragon whom she found but the brave huntsman, with his sword and his animals.

"Fear not, princess," he said, "for I am come to save you."

"Oh, sir," cried the maiden, "that is a noble, brave thought, but no one has yet been able to conquer the dragon, and I fear he will kill us both and these your friends. I pray you leave."

"I will not leave," said the huntsman stoutly, "and I will not fail as the others have failed. Come—" and he led the princess into the chapel, and locked the door and barred it.

No sooner had he done so than the dragon appeared, roaring and blowing fire from each of its seven heads. But when it saw the huntsman it pulled itself up short and said, "Where is the princess? And who are you?"

"The princess," said the huntsman, drawing his sword, "is where you cannot reach her. I am a huntsman, come to slay you for the evil you have done to this town." And with that he lunged at the dragon.

The dragon snorted sparks at the grass, to light it and burn the huntsman up—but the hare, the fox, the wolf, the bear, and the lion rushed to the burning grass and with their feet stamped out the flames.

Then the dragon gathered itself together and with a mighty leap rushed upon the huntsman—but the huntsman swung his sword high and with a single blow cut off three of the dragon's heads.

The dragon snarled in fury and spread its wings, rising up in the sky above the reach of the sword, and spat fire. But the huntsman dodged this way and that, avoiding the flames, and taunted the dragon until it lowered itself with its wings and spread its talons to seize the huntsman—whereupon the huntsman swung his sword again, cutting off three more of the dragon's fearsome heads.

Now the dragon was greatly weakened and sank down upon the ground, panting and eyeing the huntsman with evil intent. The huntsman was by now weak also, for he had used great effort thus far and the magic of the drink in the cups was lessening. So for a time the two watched each other warily, and rested. At last, with a great bellow the dragon heaved itself up again and ran toward the huntsman—but the huntsman, with the last burst of strength he could summon, smote the dragon a blow upon the tail, severing it. "My friends," he then called to his animals, "come to my aid; I can fight no longer!" As he sank upon the grass, the hare, the fox, the wolf, the bear, and the lion made an end to the dragon at last.

When the huntsman had recovered a little, he opened the chapel and found that the poor princess had fainted dead away from fright. So he carried her outside, and his animals brought water to bathe her face. At last she opened her eyes and said, "Am I slain now and in heaven?"

"No," said the huntsman, smiling at her, "this is only heaven on earth—for you are alive and the dragon is dead."

Then the maiden embraced him joyfully and said, "And you, brave huntsman, will be my own, dear husband, for so my father has decreed."

The huntsman then showed her the body of the dragon and told her how the animals had assisted him and how they had brought water for her. So the princess took off her long and many-stranded coral necklace and out of it she made a collar for each of the animals, the lion being the one to have the golden clasp on his coral collar. And then she took out her handkerchief, which had her name worked on it in silver and gold, and she gave it to the huntsman, saying, "Keep this with you always." And the huntsman cut out the dead dragon's seven tongues, cleaned them, and wrapped them with care in the handkerchief.

When he was finished, he was again overcome with exhaustion and he saw that the maiden swayed a little where she stood, so he said, "Come, let us both rest." So they lay down near the chapel to sleep. "You keep watch, my lion," the huntsman said, "and wake me if anyone comes."

The lion lay down next to his master, but he, too, was weary and in need of sleep, so he called to the bear and said, "Friend bear, I must sleep awhile. Do you keep watch, and wake me if anyone comes." The bear lay beside the lion, but soon began to yawn, so he called to the wolf, saying, "Friend wolf, sleep is overtaking me; do you watch awhile, only wake me should anyone come." The wolf agreed, thinking he could easily stay awake, but after a few minutes the warm sun and soft breezes lulled him and his eyelids drooped. So he called to the fox, and said, "Friend fox, I find I am more tired than I thought; kindly come beside me here and keep watch while I nap, but wake me if anyone comes near." The fox said, "I will," and took his place, but soon found himself nodding and so he called to the hare and said, "Friend hare, I cannot keep awake; do you spell me awhile, and wake me should anyone draw near." And the hare said, "I will do my best," for well he knew that he had no one to call upon—but though he tried valiantly to keep sleep away, it soon overpowered him as well.

And now the marshal, who had been watching from afar, saw that all movement on the hill had ceased, and he stealthily climbed up to make sure that all was over, so he could report the sad news to the king. But instead of what he expected, he found the dragon slain and the princess asleep instead of dead, and asleep nearby lay the huntsman and all his beasts. Now the marshal could easily guess what had occurred, but he was an evil, selfish man, so with drawn sword he stepped over the sleeping animals, cut off the huntsman's head, and carried the sleeping maiden down the hill again. Halfway to the palace she awoke and screamed, but the marshal held her fast and said, "Not a word. I have control now, and you shall tell your father the king that it is I who killed the dragon and then you shall be my wife and I shall reign when your father is dead."

"You are an evil liar," cried the princess. "I will not marry you, nor will I tell my father other than the truth!"

So then the marshal put the maiden down and, drawing his sword again, said he would kill her if she did not do as he said. She had no choice but to say she would.

The king was overjoyed when the marshal brought him his child

and he embraced her and wept over her as the marshal stood impatiently by. When the king had done, the marshal said, "Sire, it is I who killed the dragon and saved your daughter and the village. Do you now make good your promise and give her to me in marriage."

"Did he kill the dragon?" the king asked his daughter.

"He says that he did," she said, "but I will not marry him until a year and a day from now."

"Very well," said the king, and he would not let anything the marshal said sway him.

Now while this sad scene was taking place in the palace below, upon the hill a great bumblebee came and sat on the hare's nose, waking him only long enough for him to brush it off with his paw. The bumblebee flew back, and again the hare woke only long enough to brush it off and then he fell as deeply asleep as before. The third time, the bee stung the hare and he woke up completely. "Someone is coming," he said, shaking the fox, and the fox turned to the wolf, shook him, and said, "Someone is coming," so the wolf woke the bear, saying the same, and the bear woke the lion. And the lion, who was next to his master, shook him but then saw that he was dead and the maiden gone, and he roared in anger and grief and said to the bear, "Why did you not wake me?" and the bear turned to the wolf and said, "Scoundrel, why did you not wake me?" and the wolf demanded of the fox the same, and the fox of the hare, and the poor hare did not know what to say, for he had no one to turn to. "Friend hare," they all shouted, "what have you to say for yourself?"

"Alas," said the hare, "I know not—although I do not think I did any worse than the rest of you." They all moved closer to him angrily, so the hare quickly raised his paw and said, "The chief thing is our master, not me or my fault; I know where there is a root that can make him whole again."

"Run and get it," roared the lion, "and be back within one day."

The hare ran as swift as lightning and was back within a day. Then the lion put the huntsman's head near his body, and the hare put the magic root in the huntsman's mouth, and all the animals stepped back in wonder, for the huntsman's neck healed itself, and the animals rejoiced.

Then the huntsman looked around and said, "But where is the princess?" so the animals had to say that she was gone. And the huntsman grieved mightily but saw there was naught to be done.

He gathered his animals around him and they traveled the world, earning their bread and passing the time by dancing for people who marveled to see a hare, a fox, a wolf, a bear, and a lion dancing with a man.

At the end of one year, the huntsman's travels brought him back to the same town, and he saw red banners hanging from all the houses instead of the black crepe that had been there when he had first arrived. He sought out the same inn and, when he had provided for his animals and secured his room, he said to the innkeeper, "Why is the town decked with banners? Is there a celebration, or has the king won a war?"

"Ah," said the innkeeper, "a celebration. The king's daughter, who last year was to be fed to the dragon, is to be married tomorrow to the man who delivered her—the king's marshal, who bravely slew the beast."

Aha! thought the huntsman, hatred for the evil marshal flooding his heart. But all he said was, "Is that so?" and went to bed.

The next day, however, when the huntsman sat down for his noonday meal, he sighed and said, "Ah, this is all very good, but what I really crave is bread from the king's baker."

The innkeeper smiled and said, "Yes, who would not crave that, for it is the best in the land. But mine is more than passable, as you may remember." And he cut a slice off the loaf he had put before the huntsman.

But the huntsman pushed it away and said, "No offense, innkeeper, but I will have bread from the king's baker."

"Will you?" said the innkeeper, smiling once again. "I will bet you one hundred gold pieces that you cannot get any."

"Truly?" asked the huntsman.

"Truly," said the innkeeper. "Here is my purse on it."

"Well," said the huntsman, "then here is mine," and he laid on the table a purse with one hundred gold pieces in it, for he had been saving his gold for just such a time. Then he called his hare and said, "Friend hare, go to the king's daughter and ask her for some bread from her father's baker."

Alas, thought the poor hare, had he asked the lion, the lion would have asked the bear, and had he asked the bear, the bear would have asked the wolf, and had he asked the wolf, the wolf would have asked the fox—and any of them could fight the dogs that run through the streets of this town—but he asked me, and so I must go as best I can. So the poor little hare ran like the wind through the streets, and he just managed to stay away from the town dogs, and duck into the king's palace just ahead of their barking noses. Once he was inside, he hid under the princess's chair, and when he had caught his breath, he scratched gently at her foot. The princess, thinking he was one of her pets, said, "No, no! Go away." So the hare scratched again and went on till she looked and saw him, and was about to exclaim, "Goodness, a hare!" and call a servant to remove him, when she saw his coral collar and her heart leaped in joy. She picked the hare up in her arms and carried him to her room, and stroking him gently said, "Dearest of hares, your master must have sent you."

"That is true," said the hare. "My master wants bread from the king's baker."

"Well," said the princess, "he shall have it," for though she did not understand what the huntsman was up to, she trusted him.

Accordingly, she sent for the king's baker and when he had brought a fresh, warm loaf, the hare said, "Please, princess, ask him to carry it for me, for if I must run with it, I will be too slow and the dogs will catch me." So the princess ordered the baker to go with the hare as far as the inn door. At the door the baker left and the hare carried the bread in to his master, who put it on the table, happily, knowing now that the king's daughter remembered him. To the astonished innkeeper he said, "Here is the king's bread, my friend. Your hundred gold pieces are now mine."

"Yes, you must be right," said the innkeeper, sniffing the bread's fine aroma, "for no one bakes bread this fragrant except the king's baker." And he pushed his purse across the table to the huntsman.

But the huntsman ignored it and said, "Now that I have the bread, I wish I had some of the king's roast meat to eat with it."

The innkeeper smiled and said, "That I would like to see, but I cannot afford to bet you for it."

"I will try without betting," said the huntsman, and he called the fox and said, "Friend fox, I would have some of the king's roast meat. Kindly go to the king's daughter and ask her for some."

Now the fox was not overfond of dogs, either, but he was used to dodging them and managed to get to the palace without being noticed. And

like the hare he hid under the princess's chair. He licked her foot gently till she noticed him, and recognized his collar.

"Dearest of foxes," she said, carrying him to her room, "what has your master sent you for?"

"Roast meat," said the fox, "some of the king's roast meat."

So the princess called the cook, who brought out a piece of juicy beef cooked to such a turn that it made the fox's mouth water. "The cook had better carry it," he said, "for surely the town dogs will want it as soon as they smell it—and I must say, I am tempted myself." So the cook carried the roast as far as the inn door, and then the fox carried it in to his master.

"Well done, friend fox," said the huntsman with joy.

The innkeeper was again astonished, but as soon as he saw how skillfully the roast was cooked, he was sure it was from the king's kitchen.

"And now," said the huntsman, "I must have some vegetables to go with my meat. Wolf!" he called, and when the wolf came to him, he asked him to fetch him some vegetables cooked as the king liked them.

The wolf was afraid of no one, man or beast, so he strolled calmly to the palace while people fled from him in alarm. He found the princess alone in her sitting room, where he brushed gently against her leg.

"Dearest of wolves," she said, touching his coral collar, "what is it that your brave master wants?"

"Some vegetables, if you please," answered the wolf, "cooked the way the king likes them."

So the princess called the cook, and ordered the king's favorite vegetable dish. When it was ready the cook carried it as far as the inn door, and the wolf took it in to his master.

"This is fine as far as it goes," said the huntsman, after thanking the wolf and rejoicing silently in the princess's love and loyalty. "But a bit of pastry would be nice afterward." So he called for the bear, and he said, "Friend bear, you are as fond of sweets as I, so you will understand. Kindly go to the princess and bring back whatever dessert the king likes best."

As the bear went through the streets, the townspeople trembled in their locked houses, and when he reached the palace the guardsmen tried to stop him, but he boxed them on the ears and they fell back in fright. He went inside and hid until the princess was alone and then he growled softly and she saw his collar and said, "Dearest of bears, what may I give you for your master?" The bear told her, and she called for the king's confectioner, who provided a beautiful cake decorated with spun sugar and candied fruits and, as the bear looked longingly at it, the princess ordered the confectioner to carry it to the inn. But as the bear was taking the dish from the confectioner, one or two of the candied fruits came loose and fell to the ground, so the bear licked them quickly up.

"Thank you, friend bear," said the huntsman, his eyes twinkling when he saw there were two fruits missing from the pattern on the cake. But he did not mention it. To the innkeeper he said, "What a fine meal, is it not? And yet no banquet is complete without wine." So he called the lion to him and said, "Friend lion, kindly go to the king's daughter and ask her for some of her father's wine—but be sure it is the king's and not some underling's, for I understand he has his own private stock."

With great dignity the lion walked through the streets, his magnificent tail swinging slowly from side to side, and while he walked, no one moved. When he got to the palace, one or two of the bravest guardsmen tried to bar his way, so he roared once softly, and they ran away. The lion went straight to the princess's room and for a moment this time she was afraid. But then she saw his coral collar with its gold clasp and said, "Dearest of lions, what does your master wish?"

"Some wine," said the lion, "the kind the king drinks."

So the princess called the king's cupbearer and told him to bring the lion some of the king's wine, but the lion said, "I will go with him to make sure he gets it right."

The cupbearer took the lion into the common cellar, where the wine that the servants drank was kept, and began to draw some out from a keg into a bottle. But the lion held up a paw and said, "Draw me some first, cupbearer, for I must taste it for my master."

The cupbearer then took a goblet and filled it and gave it to the lion. He took one swallow and then, making a terrible face, threw the rest upon the ground. "This cannot be the king's wine," he said, angrily switching his tail. "Let me have some of the best."

But the cupbearer still did not see how an animal could tell one wine from another, so he went to another part of the common cellar and drew off a goblet full of the wine drunk by the king's courtiers.

"Better," said the lion, draining nearly half the wine but pouring the rest upon the ground, "but not the king's, I'll wager."

"Oh, but it is," lied the cupbearer—but the lion both boxed his ears and roared, and so at last the cupbearer took the lion into the king's private cellar and drew him some of the best.

"Ah," said the lion, "that could well be the king's wine," and he drank all the wine in the goblet right down. Then he told the cupbearer to fill half a dozen bottles and help him carry them to the inn door in a basket, which the cupbearer did.

When the huntsman had thanked the lion, he turned to the innkeeper and said, "Here now is a true feast, exactly like the king's. And now I will enjoy it with you and with my faithful animals." So he made a place for the innkeeper and called in all his beasts, and the animals sat down with the two men and ate and drank merrily—the hare, the fox, the wolf, the bear, and the lion; the innkeeper and the huntsman. And the huntsman was the merriest of all, for he knew that his game had proved the princess remembered him and loved him still.

When they had finished, the huntsman rose and said, "Well, innkeeper, you have seen me eat and drink as the king eats and drinks. Now you will see me go to the palace and marry the king's daughter."

"Now, that I will never see," said the innkeeper, "for the princess is to marry the king's marshal—he who slew the dragon—this very day."

"You are right," said the huntsman, "and you are wrong. The princess will certainly marry the dragon-slayer, though whether it will be this very day I cannot be sure. But I am sure of this: The princess will not marry the king's marshal."

"Ha, ha," laughed the innkeeper. "Cleverly said, but they are one and the same, the dragon-slayer and the king's marshal."

"Is that so?" said the huntsman.

"It must be so," said the innkeeper, "for everyone says it. I will stake my inn on it."

So the huntsman drew out another purse full of gold—for he had spent so little of that which had appeared under his pillow—and put it on the table. "A thousand gold pieces," he said. "That is my stake on it."

Now at this very moment, the king and his daughter were having a quiet talk by themselves before the wedding, and the king said to his daughter, "What were all those animals that were about the palace today? I am told they came to you, and that you sent each away again with one of my cooks and a basket or a covered dish."

"I may not tell you, Father," said the princess, "at least not yet. But if you will send to the inn and have the animals' master brought here, you will learn the truth."

And so the king sent a messenger to the inn and the messenger arrived as the huntsman and the innkeeper were still arguing over who had killed the dragon. When the messenger stated his business, the huntsman got up and said, "You see, innkeeper, it is beginning to fall out as I predicted. Now," he said to the messenger, "I cannot go before the king dressed in these common clothes! Do you go back to your master and your mistress the princess and bring me suitable garments, and also a coach and horses to convey me, and servants to see to my needs along the way."

The messenger did not believe that these wishes would be granted but he relayed them to the king, who turned to his daughter in amazement and said, "What is all this? What should I do?"

"Do as he wishes, Father," said the princess, smiling.

So the king sent the messenger back with clothes and a coach and horses and servants, and the innkeeper's mouth dropped wide open when he saw them driving into his courtyard.

Soon the huntsman was shown into the palace, and his animals, who had come with him, were shown in as well, for he would not leave them outside. By now the wedding entertainment had begun, and the marshal was with the guests who were assembled in the Great Hall of the palace—but the marshal did not recognize the huntsman in his fine clothes.

When the huntsman was seated in a place of honor near the king, as the princess requested, seven servants came in bearing the dragon's seven severed heads. The king stood up and said to the guests, "Behold, these are the heads of the evil dragon that my marshal slew one year and one day ago. And because he slew the dragon and saved the town from destruction and my child from death, I will today give him my daughter's hand in marriage. And he will rule after me."

The guests all clapped and drew in their breath to see how huge and fierce the dragon's heads were—but the huntsman stood up, and, before anyone could stop him, he had pried open the dragon's mouths. "Where," he said, facing the marshal, "are the dragon's seven tongues?"

The marshal grew pale, and his knees shook, and because he could think of nothing else, he said, "Dragons do not have tongues."

The huntsman said, "I wish liars did not have tongues, either. But dragons do have tongues, and this one's have remained with its slayer." Then he took out the princess's handkerchief, which he had carefully guarded during the year and a day, and he put each tongue in its proper mouth and all present saw that each tongue fit. Then he held up the handkerchief, which had the princess's name on it in silver and gold, and said to the princess, "To whom did you give this, your highness?"

She answered, "To the brave man who killed the dragon."

Then the huntsman called his animals one by one and took the coral collars off each except the lion and said to the princess, "Whose are these bits of coral?"

"They were mine," she replied. "Together they formed a necklace I wore on the day I was to go to the dragon, but I cut the necklace and gave a piece to each of the animals who helped slay the dragon. The lion has the piece with the clasp." And she pointed to it, still around his neck.

"I slept," said the huntsman, turning to the king, "after I had killed the dragon, and your daughter slept also, as did my animals, for they helped me bravely, and we all were weary. And your marshal came to us, and carried off your daughter and made her say it was he who had killed the dragon. He thought he had killed me, too, but my animals cured me with a magic root, and when I saw that the princess was gone, I despaired and left the kingdom. But when I came back and heard that she was to be married today to this faithless coward, I sent my animals to her one by one to prove that I was alive and had come for her."

The king turned to his daughter and asked, "Is this true?"—but he could see by the love in the princess's eyes that it was.

"Yes, Father," she said, "it is true. The marshal said he would kill me if I told the truth, and that is why I asked you to delay my marriage for a year and a day. I hoped that by then my brave huntsman would find his way to me again, and that we would find a way of showing you the truth."

The king believed her, and on that same day the huntsman and the princess were married, and the marshal was seized and tried before four wise judges, who had him executed. The young king-to-be had his father and foster-father brought to the palace—but his twin brother was nowhere to be found. Later he sent for the innkeeper and said, "Innkeeper, what do you think? You see I have married the king's daughter."

"Alas," said the innkeeper, "happy for you and sad for me, for I cannot ask you to allow me to back down on a wager. According to that, my inn is yours."

"But according to fairness, it is not," said the young king-to-be. "I have all I need, as you can see." And he let the innkeeper keep his inn and gave him the purses of gold as well.

The young king- and queen-to-be lived happily together, though the princess often had to stay at home and occupy herself alone with needlework and singing and other queenly pastimes while her husband was out hunting—for king though he would someday be, the huntsman was still a huntsman at heart.

There was a certain forest nearby into which no one went, for it was enchanted, and no one who had gone into it had ever come out again. But it was so lush and beautiful that the huntsman-prince gave his father-in-law the king no rest until he had agreed to let him hunt in it. One morning the huntsman rode forth with his animals and his attendants and when he came to the forest, he saw a beautiful deer—a hind. He bade his attendants wait for him while he hunted it, for he knew they were afraid to go into the forest. The attendants stayed at the edge of the forest until sunset, but their master did not return. Much afraid, they rode sadly home, and the king and his daughter were distraught when they heard the news.

Meanwhile, the hind led the huntsman and his beasts a merry chase, just showing itself long enough so they knew where it was, and then leaping into the brush again, so that they lost sight and scent of it. But then it would appear again, and lead them still deeper into the forest. As evening fell, the huntsman resigned himself to having lost the hind and blew upon his hunting horn, so his attendants might hear it and answer with theirs. But there was no answer; his attendants were too far away to hear.

The huntsman was wise enough to know it would be useless to try to find his way out of the forest at night, so he got down from his horse, gathered wood, lit himself a cozy fire, and prepared to spend the night with his animals huddled around him for warmth.

Just as they had all settled themselves, there came a faint sound as if from above the huntsman's head, and it sounded like a human voice.

The huntsman looked around, but, as he saw nothing, he lay down to sleep again. But the noise came once more, this time louder, and this time when the huntsman looked he saw an old woman perched in a tree nearby. "Oh, I am so cold!" the woman moaned. "So cold—so cold!"

"Well, climb down, grandmother," the huntsman called, "and join us at our fire."

"No, no," the woman cried. "I am afraid of your animals. They will bite me."

"Nonsense," said the huntsman. "They have bitten no one yet, except a dragon whom they helped me slay."

"Still," said the woman—who was a witch—"I dare not. But I will throw you down a wand, and if you strike your animals on the back with it, they will not hurt me."

"Very well," said the huntsman, for he wanted to sleep and the old woman was keeping him awake.

The witch threw down a wand, and the huntsman struck each animal gently on the back with it, and when he had struck them all, to his horror, he saw them turn to stone. But as soon as he saw that, the witch was already at his side, laughing, and she struck him with the wand, which he had dropped, and he was turned to stone also. Then the witch used her magic to take the huntsman and his animals to her cave, where there were other stone-people and stone-beasts lying all around.

Days passed, and when the huntsman still did not return to his young wife, she grew more anxious every day. While the huntsman lay helpless in the enchanted forest, his own twin brother arrived in the kingdom. He, too, had danced with his animals for a living. But after more than a year, he wondered how his younger brother was faring and so he had returned to the tree into which they had plunged the knife. When he got to it, he saw that the side of the blade facing where his brother had gone was half-rusted, half-bright. "Perhaps I can still save him," he said to himself, "for it is after all only *half*-rusted." He called to his animals and they traveled west, and soon came to the town at the foot of the hill. At the gate of the town the king's guard met him and, thinking he was the princess's husband, for he looked just like him and had the same animals, asked, "Shall I run ahead, your highness, and tell the princess and the king that you are safely home? They have been afraid for you, since you have been in the enchanted forest for so long."

The older huntsman immediately realized that the guard was speaking of his younger brother, but thought it wise to learn more before he told anyone who he was. "Yes," he said, "run ahead and announce me."

He followed the guard to the palace and was met by the king and his daughter, and when the princess, embracing him, said, "But why did you stay away so long?" he answered, again carefully, "I became lost in the forest, and have spent all this time finding my way out again."

That evening there was a great feast in honor of his return, and his animals were petted and fed dainties, and then the princess took him to the room she shared with her husband. But the older huntsman would not go to bed, saying that he would prefer to sit by the window instead.

The next day the older huntsman asked as many questions as he dared about the enchanted forest and finally he said to the king, "I must go back there again to hunt." The king at first refused, but then the huntsman said, "Sire, I must prove my courage by going back to the very place that nearly conquered me." So the king, with misgivings, let him go.

As soon as he entered the forest, the older huntsman saw the white hind, who led him deeper and deeper under the trees until night fell. So he lit a fire and sat down beside it with his animals to rest. No sooner had he sat down than he heard a voice above him moaning, "Oh, oh, I am so very cold," and he looked up and saw the same old woman his brother had seen.

"Come down, little grandmother," he said, "and you may warm yourself at my fire."

"Oh, no, I cannot. Your animals will bite me," she replied.

"They will not bite you," said the huntsman, affectionately stroking his wolf, who lay with his head in his master's lap.

"I am afraid nonetheless," said the witch, "but I will throw down a wand for you to strike them with and then they will not bite me."

"Strike my faithful animals?" cried the huntsman. "Never!" And then, laying the wolf gently aside, he said, "Come down out of that tree!"—for by now he suspected she was not what she seemed.

"I will not!" she cried in alarm. "What do you want of me?"

"Never mind that," he replied. "Only come down, or I will shoot you," and he raised his gun.

But the witch laughed at that, and said, "Go ahead. Your bullets cannot harm me."

Then he was sure she was a witch and, to prove it, he fired, and the bullets went right through her. Then, knowing that even though bullets of lead are no use against witches, bullets of silver are, he tore the silver bullets off his coat, loaded his gun with them, and fired once more.

With a scream, the witch dropped out of the tree.

"And now, old witch," he said, catching her—for he had only nicked her, on purpose—"tell me where my brother is or it will go ill with you."

The witch was now so frightened that she said instantly, "He is in my cave, turned to stone."

"Take me there," the huntsman ordered, and he slipped his belt around her like a leash and made her lead him.

When they got to the cave, the older huntsman looked around and was sorely grieved to see his younger brother and all his animals and many other people as well all turned to stone. His own animals sniffed their brothers and nudged them sadly with their noses.

"Now, old witch, turn my brother and all the creatures here into themselves again. I have two silver bullets left, and this time they will find their mark!"

So the witch touched each stone creature with her wand and turned them all back to life again.

The two brothers embraced, and their animals embraced also in their various ways, and all around them stood grateful shepherds and shop-keepers, woodcutters and foresters, blacksmiths, and all manner of other folk, and they thanked the older huntsman heartily for delivering them. Then they bound the witch with stout cords and gave her to a constable whom she had also enchanted, and he carried her away on his horse, who had come to life along with the shepherds' sheep and the hunting dogs and the other animals that the witch had also turned to stone. As soon as the witch was out of the forest, it was no longer enchanted.

Then the two brothers went back to the palace, but they walked slowly, telling each other their adventures. The younger said, finishing his story after the older finished his, "And so the king gave me his daughter's hand in marriage and I am to rule after him."

"Yes," said his brother, "I saw that when I arrived, for the guard bowed to me and asked if he should tell the king and princess that I—he meant you—had returned. And, of course, the princess embraced me fondly when I arrived, and we had a great feast with the king, and after-ward I had to spend the night in your room."

At those words the younger huntsman was consumed with jealousy and so angry that he put his hand on his sword. But his reason returned quickly and he said to himself, "Would I kill the man who has rescued me?" and he decided to wait and see how the princess acted when they returned to the palace—whether she would love his brother now, or him.

"Since you look just like me," he said, as they approached the pal-ace, "let us go into the town by opposite gates so that we will arrive at the palace at the same time but from different directions."

The older brother agreed, and they parted, and each approached the palace from the opposite direction.

Soon two different watchmen reported to the king, at the same time, in the same words: "The prince, the prince returns!"—only one of them said "from the east" and the other said "from the west."

"That cannot be," said the king.

But then the two brothers marched solemnly into the courtyard, one from the west side and the other from the east, and their animals came after them, and they stood before the king.

The king looked in amazement and then said to his daughter, "Which is your husband? One of them must be an imposter!"

The princess looked from one to the other as well, and could not tell the difference. But then she spied something pink in the lion's mane, tipped with something gold, and she bent down and unfastened it. "This man is my husband," she cried, going to the younger huntsman. "The man whom this lion follows is he—for his lion wears my necklace still."

Then the younger huntsman, laughing, embraced his bride, and said, "Yes, I am your husband—and that is my twin brother, and all these animals are brothers, too."

Then the two human brothers told their story, and they all made merry till the small hours. That night when the princess and her husband went to their room, the princess said, "And are you going to sit up all night as you did last night, gazing out of the window?"

What little jealousy was left in the prince vanished at this and he smiled and said, "No, I shall not watch by the window tonight." And all was peaceful from then on between the prince and princess, and between the two brothers, and throughout the kingdom.

ALLERLEIRAUH

Once upon a time there was a queen who had golden hair that shone like a thousand suns. She was so beautiful people held their breath when they saw her. But, sad to say, this queen fell ill when she was still young and had only one child, a pretty daughter. After a few weeks had passed, she knew that she was doomed, so she called her husband the king to her bedside. Gently laying her hand in his, she said, "My love, the time may soon come when you want to marry again. But heed my wish: Do not marry anyone less beautiful than I, or anyone whose hair is less golden."

The king, weeping, promised that he would not, and at this the queen drew her last breath.

Years went by, and the queen's pretty daughter grew to near-womanhood, and still the king had no desire to marry, for he felt nothing for any woman he saw, so in love was he with the memory of his wife. In time the king's advisers, hearing the people in the kingdom grumbling about there being no queen, went to the king, bowed low, and with grave faces said, "Your majesty, we have respected your grief for lo, these many years. But the people long for a queen, and you yourself must be lonely. We propose that you send messengers throughout your kingdom and beyond to find a woman equaling or—though this be impossible—even surpassing your late wife in beauty, and that you marry her."

The king frowned, for he still did not like to think of this. But his advisers had struck one true chord: He was indeed lonely. And so in the end he said, "Very well. But remember to bring me no one who is less beautiful than my queen, and no one whose hair does not shine like a thousand suns."

"We will not, your majesty," the king's advisers promised, and they then called for the king's messengers, and sent them throughout the kingdom and beyond. But they found no one, and one by one came home alone.

Now the king's daughter had a birthday not long after the last messenger had returned, and during the festivities the king looked closely at the guests, and saw that every one of them, man and woman alike, held their breath when they saw her beauty—and, indeed, the girl was not only truly beautiful, but also had been growing more like her dead mother every day. Then the king looked more closely at her and saw that her golden hair shone like a thousand suns, and it was suddenly as if his late wife stood before him. He called his advisers and said, "Rejoice, for I have found a young woman who is as beautiful as my wife, and whose hair is as golden, and I will marry her."

"Splendid, your majesty!" cried the oldest of his advisers in great relief. "And who might she be?"

"My daughter," said the king—and the oldest adviser grew pale, and looked at his fellows, and they were pale also. "Your majesty," he said, "most noble sire, you cannot do that!"

"And why not?" asked the king. "I can do what I like. I am king."

"Sire," said the adviser, going down on his knees, "I beg you, do not even consider this, for God forbids it. A man, even if he be king, cannot marry his own daughter. Only evil can come of it. The people of your kingdom want a queen, it is true, but they are good people, and they will not accept this—it is a crime."

"I will change the laws," said the king, "and it will no longer be a crime. Now go—tell one of the footmen to fetch my daughter and bring her to me that I might tell her."

The advisers left, but the oldest went to the king's daughter and said, "Alas, princess, your father, seeing that you resemble your late mother and are indeed as beautiful and have hair as golden, wishes to marry you."

The girl stared in horror at the old man; she could not at first take in his words. But when she had understood them, she turned away for a time, and thought, and then turned back to him and said calmly, "Do not fear; it shall not be." Then she went to her father and curtsied, and said, "I have heard your wish, but before I grant it, I must have some new clothes—three dresses, one as gold as the sun, one as silver as the moon, and one that shines like the stars. And in addition to the dresses, you must get for me a hooded cloak of fur, but the fur must be of a thousand different kinds. Each kind of animal in the kingdom must give a piece of fur to this cloak, and if there be not a thousand kinds of beasts in this kingdom, why then, go to the next." She asked this because she was sure it would be impossible to fulfill, and would therefore prevent her from having to marry her father.

But the king nodded, saying, "It shall be as you wish," and sent out his messengers again. Within a month, all had been gathered: the three dresses, one as gold as the sun, one as silver as the moon, and one that shone like the stars; and the cloak made of a thousand different kinds of fur.

When the clothes had been laid out, the king called his daughter and showed them to her, saying, "Here is what you wished. And now prepare for the wedding, for I will marry you tomorrow."

The girl nodded submissively, but she had no intention of breaking the law of both heaven and earth, nor did she wish to. That very night when everyone was sleeping, she put the three dresses into a magic nutshell along with a tiny golden spinning wheel that she had, and a tiny golden reel, and a golden ring that had been her mother's. Then she put on the hooded cloak of a thousand furs, and rubbed black soot on her hands and face. And finally, waking no one, she crept out of her father's palace and away into the night.

She walked for miles, wishing to get as far away as possible so that she would never be found. When she could walk no farther, she climbed into a hollow tree and went to sleep.

Now this tree was in a forest belonging to the king of the next kingdom, who was a good, kind man, and, when he had time, also a merry one.

When the sun rose the next day, this king was already in the forest hunting. His dogs came to the tree, sniffing and wagging their tails and barking. The king rode up with his huntsmen, following the dogs, and said, "Look into that tree, huntsmen, for methinks it is hollow, and see if some animal is hiding there."

The huntsmen obeyed, and marveled at what they saw. They told the king, "Your majesty, there is indeed a beast hiding there, but it is a beast such as we have never seen, and it is fast asleep."

"Perhaps you can capture it alive," said the king. "If it is as wondrous as you say, perhaps it will be amusing, or perhaps it needs protection, for beasts are not always kind to those who are unlike themselves."

So the huntsmen crept in silence to the tree, and threw a net around the girl, and pulled it tight. At this she awoke, and cried, "Oh, spare me, spare me! I am not what I appear to be, but am one whose mother is dead and whose father would do her evil; please do not hurt me, but take me with you."

So the huntsmen reported this to the king, who said, "Let us take the beast to the palace; perhaps it can be of use in the kitchen, since you say it can talk. We cannot let the poor creature wander alone in the forest, whatever it is." And so the girl, still in her furry, hooded cloak, was taken to the palace kitchen. The king forgot all about her, being sore pressed with affairs of state, but the cook called her "Allerleirauh," which means "of all kinds of hair."

"You can live here, hairy creature," the cook said, and he pointed to a dark closet. "And you can fetch water for me, and sweep the hearth, and wash the floor, and pick and clean the vegetables."

And so the princess, now called Allerleirauh, lived in another king's palace, but in the depths of it, and did all the unpleasant and difficult jobs in the kitchen. She slept every night in her dark closet, and in it she hid the magic nutshell she had carried with her.

At last a day came when the king, his state matters now settled, gave a ball and a banquet. Allerleirauh said to the cook, "Oh, please, sir,

could I not creep upstairs during the dancing and watch, just for a little while? I will hide behind the door and no one will see me."

"I suppose," said the cook, "but mind that no one does see you. And be sure you return in no more than half an hour, for the hearth must be swept, and the king's bread soup made, and more wood brought in."

Allerleirauh thanked the cook and ran quickly into her little closet, where she took off the cloak of a thousand furs for the first time in many a day, and cleaned the soot from her hands and face. She opened the magic nutshell and put on her dress that was as gold as the sun, and when she went upstairs she had no need to hide behind the door for she was so beautiful all those who saw her held their breath, and her hair shone brighter than her dress, like a thousand suns. When the king saw her, he took her for a princess, as indeed she was, and would let no one else dance with her. There is no one so beautiful, the king thought as they danced, or so gentle. But all too soon for him the dance was over, and Allerleirauh, knowing that a half hour had surely passed, curtsied and ran out of the room, and no one could find her.

She ran back to her closet and returned the lovely dress to its nutshell, and made herself again into the hairy animal that all believed her to be. Then she returned to the kitchen and picked up her broom to sweep the hearth. "How was the ball?" asked the cook, and she replied, "Splendid—oh, it was beautiful, with many beautiful ladies and noble gentlemen, all glittering as they danced."

So the cook put off his apron and said, "If a creature like you can watch a ball, so can I. Here—you may make the bread soup for the king while I go up for a while and watch the ball. Take care you do not let any of your shaggy hairs fall into the soup, or you will have nothing but water to eat for longer than you will like."

The cook then left, and Allerleirauh set about making the bread soup for the king. When it was simmering, she went to her closet and fetched the golden ring from the magic nutshell. Just before the king's footman came for his soup, she slipped the ring into the king's bowl.

Upstairs the dancing had given way for the moment to feasting, and the king ate his soup with great relish, for he had never tasted better. When it was nearly gone, his spoon knocked against the golden ring and he brought it out in surprise and called for the cook.

"Allerleirauh," said the cook, frightened to be summoned before the king, "you must have dropped hairs in the soup after all. If it turns out that you have, not only shall you have nothing but water for longer than you like, but I will beat you as well." Then he went up to see the king.

"Cook," said the king, "who is it that made this soup?"

"I did, your majesty," said the cook in a small, terrified voice—for he feared it would go worse with him if the king knew he had entrusted its making to a mere beast.

"That cannot be," said the king, "for it tasted different from before."

The cook saw that the king had guessed the truth and, as he feared the king had disliked the soup, he said eagerly, "You are right, your majesty; it was the hairy animal whom you took from the tree that made it."

The king was surprised, but he remembered the beast now that it had been mentioned, and he said, "Send the creature to me. The soup was delicious."

So the cook went down to the kitchen and told Allerleirauh that the king wished to see her. "Be careful what you say," he said, "or it will go badly with you." But in his heart he was relieved, for the king did not seem angry, and had said he liked the soup.

"Who are you?" the king asked, when Allerleirauh knelt before him.

"I am one," said Allerleirauh, "whose mother is dead and whose father would do her evil."

"And what are you good for in the kitchen?" asked the king.

"To sweep and fetch, and to have boots thrown at me," she said.

"Now, hairy creature," said the king, "where did you get the ring that I found in my soup?"

"What ring?" said Allerleirauh. "I know nothing of that."

So the king knew little more than he had before, and he sent Allerleirauh away and forgot about her again, having other things on his mind.

When his burdens eased, the king again decided to give a ball and a banquet, and Allerleirauh again asked the cook for permission to go up and watch. "You may," said the cook, "but come back in half an hour so you can again make the king his bread soup—for clearly he likes your recipe best."

So Allerleirauh went quickly to her closet and washed, put on the dress that was as silver as the moon, and ran upstairs to the ball. And again everyone thought she was a princess, and the king went to her immediately, holding out his hand and saying, "How glad I am that you have come again," and they danced together. But when the half hour was nearly up, the dance ended, and Allerleirauh again ran away as quickly as before. No one could find her, though the king asked all his servants and all the guardsmen outside. Allerleirauh went to her closet and put on her cloak of a thousand furs, hid her little golden spinning wheel under it, and made her face and hands black. Then she returned to the kitchen to make the soup. When the footman came for it, she slipped her little golden spinning wheel into the king's bowl.

The king liked the soup as much as before, and he called for the cook, who again told him that Allerleirauh had made it. And so the king sent for Allerleirauh, who answered all his questions just as she had before, so that the king again knew no more than he had known before.

In time, the king gave a third ball and banquet, and again Allerleirauh put on a beautiful dress—this time the one that shone like the stars—and went to the ball and danced with the king. But this time, as the king whirled Allerleirauh around and around in the dance, he slipped a golden ring on her finger, and she never noticed. When the time was up and Allerleirauh wanted to leave, the king tried to hold her by the hands, but she managed to pull away even so, and run to her closet. This time, however, she was so late that she did not have time to take off her dress, so she put the cloak of a thousand furs on over it, and hid her little golden reel under it. She covered her face and hands with soot as best she could—but in her haste, she left one finger unblackened. Then she ran to the kitchen and made bread soup for the king. And, as before, the king sent for the cook, and then had the cook send for Allerleirauh.

"Did you make this soup, hairy beast?" he asked her.

"I did, sire," she answered, kneeling as before.

"And tell me again what it is that you are good for?"

"To sweep and fetch, sire, and to have boots thrown at me."

"And where," asked the king, "did you get this tiny reel that I found in my soup?"

"Sire," said Allerleirauh, "I know nothing of that."

"You have told me," said the king, "that you are one whose mother is dead and whose father would do you evil, and you speak as if you were human, not a beast. So let us see." And he came closer still, and raised her up, and saw her white finger and the ring upon it. At this, Allerleirauh became frightened and tried to twist away from him, but as she did, her cloak fell open and revealed the star-bright dress underneath.

And then the king slipped the hood of the cloak off her head, and her golden hair shone as bright as a thousand suns.

"You are human indeed," he said in wonder, calling for water with which to wash her face and hands, "and now you must tell me your story, and why you are so frightened to show who you really are."

So the girl told the king her story, and he listened in great sympathy, and allowed her to live on at the palace as a true princess instead of as a hairy animal. And in time she grew to love him, and he, her—and so they were married and lived happily ever after.

THE GOOSE GIRL

ALAS, there is great cruelty in the world, both to people and to beasts, and it, as in this story, is sad to read about.

Once there was an elderly queen who ruled over her land alone, for her husband had been dead for many years. Now this queen had a beautiful daughter whom she loved very much, and who was engaged to be married to a prince who lived far away. It was not the queen's wish to prevent her child's happiness, so when the time came for the wedding, though the queen herself was too ill to go, she made her daughter presents of many jewels, and cups and plates of gold and silver, and chains of costly metals, and necklaces and rings, and many fine, silken dresses. All this she packed in great chests for her daughter, and ordered that her daughter's horse Falada be prepared for the journey, plus horses to pull the carts laden with the jewels, dresses, and other costly items, plus a horse for her daughter's attendant.

When the time came for her child to leave, the elderly queen made her own finger bleed by pricking it with a needle. She let three drops of blood fall upon a snow white handkerchief and gave it to her daughter, saying, "Keep this with you always, for it will help you along your way." And then she sent her daughter forth, attended by one of her own maids-in-waiting.

Now this maid-in-waiting was evil and false, and jealous of the queen's daughter, for she wished to be in her place. After the two had ridden for a great distance, the princess felt thirsty. When they came to a running brook, the princess said to the maid, "Please climb down off your horse, and fetch me some water in my golden cup, for I am perishing with thirst."

"Get your own water," replied the maid sullenly—though the cup was tied to her saddle. "It is your mother who thinks I should serve you, not I myself."

The princess did not know what to make of this, for she had never heard a servant speak thus. Perhaps she is just tired and impatient, she thought, and she got down off Falada herself. But she had to scoop up the water with her hands, for the maid would not give her the golden cup.

As the princess bent over the brook and cupped her hands, she sighed, and the three drops of blood upon her handkerchief answered:

Thy mother's heart would broken be,
If this cruel treatment she could see.

The princess felt comforted by this, and mounted Falada in silence and rode on.

The sun rose high in the sky, and warmed the woods through which the princess rode with the maid, and soon there was little air to breathe among the trees, it was so hot. Again the princess felt thirsty and once more when they came to a brook, the princess said, "Good my maid, please climb down off your horse and fetch me some water in my golden cup, which is still strapped to your saddle."

But the maid replied, "Get your own water; you may serve yourself, for I have no wish to serve you."

This time the princess wept at the maid's harsh words and at her withholding of the cup. As she bent over the brook, the three drops of blood on her handkerchief said again:

Thy mother's heart would broken be,
If this cruel treatment she could see.

This time, as the princess drank from the brook, the handkerchief fell into the water and floated away, but she was weeping too much to see it. But the waiting maid saw it and smiled evilly to herself, thinking, Now I have her, for she no longer is in her mother's protection, and I may do as I like with her.

And so as the princess went back to mount her horse again, the waiting maid said, "I shall ride Falada, and you may ride my nag." Though the princess wanted to protest, she found she could not. Not only did they exchange horses but also clothes, so that when they were mounted again, the waiting maid looked like a princess and the princess looked like a waiting maid.

"And now," said the waiting maid, "you must swear not to say a word of this to anyone in the palace. Speak of it to neither king nor queen nor prince nor servant—and if you do not swear, I shall kill you"—and she held a jeweled knife to the princess's throat.

"I swear," said the princess—for what else could she do?

"Furthermore," said the waiting maid, "if you break your oath at any future time, I shall know of it, and come to you wherever you are, and kill you dead."

So the poor princess was forced to ride behind her maid in silence, and to serve her in everything she ordered. There was no one else there to see what happened except the horses—and Falada, the princess's own horse, remembered it well.

When the small procession arrived at the palace, the prince ran out to meet his bride, and helped the waiting maid from her horse while all the courtiers and all the servants lined up to watch and rejoice. With great ceremony, the prince led the waiting maid inside, and left the true princess standing near the stables with the horses. But the old king the prince's father looked outside and saw the real princess standing there, and observed her beauty and her sadness. He went quickly to the room where the bride was to stay until the wedding and asked the waiting maid, "Who is the girl who stands outside near the stables?"

"Oh," said the waiting maid with a haughty air, "that is just my servant. I have no use for her now, but she should be given some task, so she will not grow lazy and fat."

The old king tried to think of some work in the palace but could think of none that was not being done already. At last he said, "She can help young Conrad, the boy who looks after my flock of geese." And so the true princess became a goose girl.

The next day the false bride said to the prince, "I wish you would do me one favor before we wed."

"And what is that?" asked the prince, taking her hand. "For you know I would do anything for you."

"That horse I rode here yesterday," said the false bride, "made me angry along the way; I wish you would have him killed." She asked that because she knew that of all the horses, Falada was the one who best remembered what had happened in the forest.

The prince was startled but he sent for the stableman to have the deed done, for he had promised he would do anything for his bride.

The real princess grieved sorely when she heard that Falada was dead, but she gave the stableman a piece of gold from one of her chests that had not yet been unpacked, and made him promise to put Falada's head on the town gate. "I pass the gate night and morning with the geese," she said, "and will be able to see him for a time still if you do what I ask."

And so the stableman took the gold, and did what the princess asked.

The next morning, when the princess drove the geese through the town gate with the boy Conrad, she said:

Falada, sadness now I see!

And the selfless Falada answered:

Alas, my queen, I'm sad for thee.
Thy mother's heart would broken be,
If this cruel treatment she could see.

Conrad noticed this, but decided that it was none of his affair, so he did not speak of it, and they went on to the meadow with the geese. When the geese were contentedly feeding, the true princess sat down on a rock and unbraided her hair, which she had not yet had time to comb, for they had left the palace early with the geese. Conrad marveled at its brightness and beauty and wanted to touch it and perhaps take one or two hairs to keep. But the princess saw what he wanted and quickly said:

Friend wind, please blow a breeze for me!
Send Conrad's hat away,
That he may chase it carefully—
Leave me in peace this day.

At once a strong wind came up and blew Conrad's hat off his head, and he had to go running after it. It took him so long to catch up to it that by the time he returned, the true princess had finished combing her hair and had braided it again. That made Conrad angry, for he could not now pluck out a few hairs to keep for himself, but he kept his anger inside and did not speak of it or of anything else on the way home.

The next morning, when Conrad and the true princess drove the geese through the town gate, the princess said:

Falada, sadness now I see!

And Falada answered:

Alas, my queen, I'm sad for thee.
Thy mother's heart would broken be,
If this cruel treatment she could see.

That day, the princess again sat down on a stone in the meadow to comb her hair and this time Conrad came up behind her and tried to pull it, but the princess said quickly:

Friend wind, please blow a breeze for me!
Send Conrad's hat away,
That he may chase it carefully—
  Leave me in peace this day.

Again Conrad had to run after his hat, and he was even angrier than before when he came back to find that the princess had braided her hair neatly again, and fastened it with pins to the top of her head. He was so angry that he went to the old king that evening and said, "You must find me another girl to help tend the geese, or let me do it alone, for I will not work with that waiting maid any longer."

"Oh?" said the old king. "And why not, pray?"

Conrad did not want to explain the true reason, so instead he said, "Well, each morning when we go through the gate she talks to that horse's head that hangs there."

"Hmm," said the old king, wondering what all this was about. "And what does she say when she talks to it?"

The boy answered, "She says:

'Falada, sadness now I see!'

And the head says:

'Alas, my queen, I'm sad for thee.
Thy mother's heart would broken be,
If this cruel treatment she could see.'

Queen, indeed!" the boy said. "It is more as if she is a witch!" Then, seeing that the king seemed sympathetic, he told him how she also commanded the wind in the meadow.

"Do as you always do tomorrow," said the old king, his brow furrowed in thought, "and I will watch and see what is what."

So the next morning, the old king hid behind the gate as Conrad and the geese and the true princess went through, and he heard with his own

Mayer

ears the exchange between the princess and Falada. And then he followed them to the meadow and saw what happened there. And then the old king, who was very wise, went away and thought some more.

That evening, when the true princess was back in the palace, the old king summoned her and said, "I know that you speak to the head of the bride's horse, and that it answers you, speaking of sadness and of your mother. And I know that the boy Conrad has taken a fancy to you, and, as boys will, wants to pull your hair, but that you call out to the wind to blow his hat away and it does. Now what is all this, child? Why does all this happen as I have described?"

"I may not tell you, your majesty," said the true princess, "for I have sworn not to, and if I tell anyone, king or queen or prince or servant, there is someone who will kill me."

"It is bad," said the wise old king, "to keep sorrows inside; if you cannot tell a person what is wrong, perhaps you can tell my old iron stove." And he pointed out the stove to her, and went away.

And so the true princess, whose sorrow was indeed heavy to bear, crawled inside the old iron stove and spoke aloud of all that had happened, and wept as if her heart would break.

But the stovepipe went through the next room on its way outside, and the old king stood next to it and heard everything she said. And when her words had changed to tears, he let her cry for a time to ease her heavy heart, and then he went in and opened the stove and lifted her out. "Come, my dear," he said kindly. "It is over." And he sent for beautiful clothes for her, and his own wife's loyal maids to help her dress, and as soon as she came before him again, it was easy to tell she was indeed a princess. Then the old king called for his son, and told him all that had happened, and the young prince was glad, for secretly he did not like the false princess; though she was beautiful, she seemed cold and unkind.

"And now," said the old king, "let us set about having the wedding without further delay."

The palace cooks prepared the wedding feast and the guests were summoned—but no one told the waiting maid what had happened, and the true princess was seated where the maid could not see her. During the course of the feast, the old king said he had a riddle to ask and he said to the waiting maid, "What punishment is fit for a servant who turns on her mistress out of jealousy and tries to take her place?"

"Oh," the waiting maid replied without thinking, "she should surely be executed."

"Ah," said the old king, "then that is what your fate will be, for you are that servant, and not only have you done this, but you have done it most cruelly."

And when that was carried out, the wedding feast went forward. A kind wizard soon restored Falada to life, and the new queen's elderly mother was sent for and brought to the palace in a fine and comfortable coach. They all lived in peace thereafter—even Conrad, who in time grew up and found himself a wife, and lived with her, happy and content, well into old age.

LITTLE RED CAP

THERE was once a little girl whom everyone loved. You may know her as "Little Red Riding Hood," but long ago when this story was first told, she was called "Little Red Cap," because of a beautiful, red velvet cap her grandmother once gave her, which she always wore.

Little Red Cap's grandmother lived in the woods, some distance from where Little Red Cap lived with her parents. She was a spry old lady, but a time came when she began to feel poorly, and Little Red Cap and her mother were worried about her. One morning, the day after baking day, Little Red Cap's mother said to her, "Wouldn't it be nice to take Grandmother the cake we made yesterday, along with a bottle of wine?"

"Oh, yes," said Little Red Cap. "That would be very nice! I will take them to her"—and she reached up to the coat hook for her cape and her red velvet cap.

"Now listen to me, Little Red Cap," said her mother fondly, helping Little Red Cap fasten her cape, "you must be very careful going through the woods all by yourself. Stay on the path, walk quickly and quietly, and be careful not to stumble, for if you drop what you are carrying, your poor grandmother will have nothing."

"I will be careful, Mother," Little Red Cap replied.

"And," said her mother, straightening the red velvet cap, "when you arrive, remember to say 'Good morning' to Grandmother politely and ask her how she is feeling."

"I promise," said Little Red Cap, and turned to go.

"Remember," her mother called after her, "stay on the path."

"I will, Mother," Little Red Cap called back. "Good-bye!"—and off she went.

In a while she reached the woods and, remembering what her mother had told her, she walked quickly and quietly along the path.

It was not long before she met a wolf—but she had never seen one before, and did not know what harm it could do, so she was not afraid.

The wolf, noticing her cap, said, "Good morning, Little Red Cap."

"Good morning, sir," said Little Red Cap, thinking he must be a friendly creature since he knew her name.

"And where are you going this fine spring day?" asked the wolf.

"To my grandmother's."

"Ah," said the wolf. "And what is it that you are carrying? Some nice goody for her, I'll warrant."

"Yes," said Little Red Cap. "Yesterday my mother and I made a cake, so I am taking it to Grandmother along with some wine, for she has been feeling poorly."

"Lucky grandmother," said the wolf, thinking how tender Little Red Cap looked and what a delicious snack she would make. "And where does your grandmother live?" he asked craftily—for the path through the forest was well traveled, and anyone could come along at any moment.

"Oh," said Little Red Cap, "straight along the path; you go on till you get to the grove of nut trees, and then Grandmother lives in the little house under the three big oaks."

"Well, well," said the wolf, "it happens that I am going that way myself. May I walk with you?"

"Yes," said Little Red Cap, for she did not think her mother would mind that.

But after a time the wolf, seeing he was just as far from getting what he wanted as when he had started, and feeling hungry enough even for the old grandmother, said, "Oh, look, Little Red Cap! Look at those lovely flowers just off the path! And listen to the birds! Oh, how can you walk so quickly along the path; you seem solemn, as if you were going to school instead of walking in the woods on a lovely spring day. Look how merry everything is—especially the flowers. See how they dance in the wind!"

Little Red Cap looked around and saw the sun shining through the trees and flowers of all colors growing all around. "Yes," she said. "Oh, how pretty it all is."

"Does your grandmother like flowers?" the wolf asked slyly. "Would you not like to pick some to take to her?"

"I would," said Little Red Cap, thinking that surely it would not be wrong to go off the path just a little, especially if she were careful not to stumble—and so she went just two steps to the side to pick a daisy that grew there in the sun—and then three steps further, for there was a lovely patch of violets—and then a few more steps, for surely that was a mayflower just under that tree. And so she went from patch to patch of woodland flowers, never noticing how far she had strayed from the path, or that the wolf was no longer waiting for her.

The wolf, indeed, had gone on ahead to Grandmother's, where he knocked at the door.

"Yes," said Grandmother. "Who is there?"

The wolf made his voice high and answered, "It is I, Grandmother—Little Red Cap. I have some cake and some wine for you. Would you open the door?"

"Just lift the latch, child," said the grandmother, "for I cannot get out of bed."

So the wolf lifted the latch, and leapt in, and ate the grandmother in one gulp. Then he put on a nightgown of hers, and a frilly nightcap, and hopped into her bed.

By then Little Red Cap had found her way back to the path and, with her bouquet of flowers added to the cake and the wine, came up to Grandmother's door and knocked.

"Yes?" said the wolf, making his voice high again, and also quavery and old-sounding. "Who is there?"

"It is I, Grandmother," Little Red Cap answered. "I have some cake and some wine for you. Would you open the door?"

"Lift the latch, child," said the wolf, "for I cannot get out of bed."

So Little Red Cap lifted the latch and, remembering what her mother had told her, she said, "Good morning, Grandmother, how are you feeling?" She put the flowers in a jug and the cake and the wine on the table. Then she went up to her grandmother's bed, but all she could see of her were two ears poking up under the frilly nightcap, and two huge eyes, and what seemed to be two hands right under the top coverlet.

"Oh, Grandmother," said Little Red Cap, "you look so odd—what big ears you have!"

"The better to hear you with, Little Red Cap," replied the wolf in Grandmother's voice.

"But what big eyes you have, Grandmother!" Little Red Cap said, stepping a bit closer.

"The better to see you with, my dear."

"But Grandmother, what big hands you have!"

"The better to hug you with, my dear," said the wolf, and the bed clothes slipped a little.

"Oh, Grandmother," said Little Red Cap, "what a big mouth you have!"

"The better to eat you with!" cried the wolf, and he jumped up and swallowed Little Red Cap whole.

Having finished such a large meal, the wolf now felt sleepy and decided he might as well stay where he was. So he lay down again, pulled up the covers, and soon was asleep, snoring more loudly than Little Red Cap's grandmother had ever snored.

"Good heavens!" said a hunter, passing by the house. "I wonder what can be wrong with the old woman. She must be ill indeed to snore so loudly. And just look—her door is open!"

And so he went inside. "Hello," he called. "Mistress, are you all right?" But there was no answer, so he went to the bed and then, seeing a bit of gray fur, he pulled down the covers and found the wolf. "So it is you!" he cried—for he had hunted the very same wolf for many a weary month—and he lifted his gun, took aim, and shot the wolf dead. But then a small sound from the wolf's stomach reached his ears, and the hunter quickly seized the grandmother's sewing scissors and cut him open. Out popped Little Red Cap, saying, "Oh, my goodness! Oh, thank you, Mr. Hunter! It was so dark and stuffy inside the wolf!"—and then, a moment later, out came Little Red Cap's grandmother—slowly, for she was still weak—and she thanked the hunter also. Then they all sat down to have some of the cake and the wine, but the hunter and Little Red Cap let the grandmother have most of it, and she soon felt much better.

"Well," said Little Red Cap to herself as the kind hunter walked her home, "Mother was right about staying on the path. I will never go off it again."

And she never did.

But one day some time later, when Little Red Cap was again going to her grandmother's, another wolf stopped her, and tried to get her to leave the path. But she walked on, quickly and quietly, without even speaking to him. After a while he fell behind as if he had given up and was leaving. But Little Red Cap was sure he would follow her nonetheless, so when she got to her grandmother's she told her about him.

"Do not be afraid," said Grandmother, who was feeling much

stronger now. "We will outsmart the wicked creature. First let us bolt the door, so that he may not come in."

So they bolted the door, and the grandmother went on making sausages, which is what she had been doing all day, and Little Red Cap helped.

In a while there came a knock at the door. "Yes," said Grandmother. "Who is there?"

"It is I: Little Red Cap," came a strange high voice. "I have some fine goodies for you. Would you open the door?"

Little Red Cap put her hand over her mouth and Grandmother almost smiled, but neither of them made a sound.

"Grandmother, Grandmother!" cried the wolf. "Let me in!"

But still neither Grandmother nor Little Red Cap spoke.

"Well," they heard the wolf say at last, "perhaps the grandmother is not home. And perhaps Little Red Cap has not yet arrived. I will just jump up on the roof and wait."

They heard him jump up and they kept very quiet until they heard him yawn. In a while, he began to snore.

"Now," whispered Grandmother, "let us very quietly put the water in which we boiled the sausages into a bucket. We will pour it into the trough that is just under the edge of the roof, and I fancy that Friend Wolf will have some interest in it when he wakes up."

So Grandmother and Little Red Cap very quietly took the water outside and filled the trough with it. Then they went back indoors to wait.

It was not long before the wolf woke up, and they heard him sniffing and snuffing. Then they heard him go to the edge of the roof—and then they heard him slip and fall, splash! into the trough.

And that was the end of him.

And, as there were no other wolves in the forest except those two, Little Red Cap and her grandmother were never troubled by them again.

THE BREMEN TOWN MUSICIANS

NOT very far from Bremen, in Germany, there was a farmer's donkey, whose job for years had been to carry his master's corn to the mill to be made into meal. But when the donkey grew old, his back swayed and his step slowed, though he tried as hard as ever to help his master.

One day the donkey heard his master say to his wife, "How sad I am—for I must put my old friend the donkey out to pasture; the only strong thing about him anymore is his wonderful bray. Now I must find a younger helper to take my corn to the mill."

Well, the donkey did not want to leave his master, but he did not want to go out to pasture either, for there was nothing to do there but eat grass all day long. He called my bray "wonderful," the donkey thought, and he said it was still strong. So I shall journey to Bremen and hire myself out as a town musician.

And so one bright morning when it was still summer, the donkey set out.

It was not long before he met a hound lying beside the road, panting and gasping as if he could not catch his breath.

"What is the trouble, friend?" the donkey asked—for he was a friendly beast who enjoyed company.

"Ah, me," said the hound sadly. "I used to be a hunting dog, but this morning my master said I am too old to hunt and must be put to sleep. Without thinking I ran away, but now I fear I will not be able to find food or earn my keep."

"Well, well," said the donkey, "what good fortune for us both! I am very much in the same position as you, and I have decided to go to Bremen and become a town musician. If you are a hunting dog you must have bayed with your pack when you were on the trail of a fox or a hare—is that so?"

"It is so," said the old dog, his tail beginning to move slowly back and forth in the grass—for he, too, enjoyed company, and he liked the donkey. "In fact"—and he struggled stiffly to his feet—"I think I can manage still." So saying, he raised his nose to the sky and bayed in such fine voice that the donkey added his own, and for a while there was such music along the road that the stones shook and the trees trembled.

"Truly marvelous!" said the donkey. "You must come with me to Bremen, friend. I am sure they will pay us well to sing duets."

So off they went along the road to Bremen.

Soon the donkey, who was taller, said, "What is that, brother, in the road?" and the hound, who had the better nose, sniffed and said, "A cat, brother, I do believe; let us proceed cautiously."

And sure enough, in a while they came to a cat, sitting in the road nervously washing his face.

"Friend," said the donkey—while the cat kept a wary eye upon the dog—"are you lost or merely resting?"

"A little of both," admitted the cat, "but most of all I am uncertain. As you can see I am no longer a kitten; in fact, I daresay I have by now gone through most of my nine lives. My eyes are not what they were, or my teeth, or my claws. What I like best is to sit by the fire and dream, but my mistress says that a cat who does not go after mice does not earn his keep, and so here I am. But what next? That is what I cannot answer."

"Well," said the donkey, "it seems to me you must come with us to Bremen, where we are to be town musicians."

"I do not mind going with you," said the cat to the donkey, "but what of him?" He inclined his head gracefully toward the dog.

"Oh, don't bother about me," said the hound, "for heaven's sake! I am too old to chase after cats, and you are too old to run away—which, if

I may tell you a secret, is what we dogs like best about chasing cats. Besides," he added, "I am through with all kinds of hunting."

"I have never known a cat who did not sing to the moon," said the donkey. "You would add a fine treble, I am sure, to my bass and the hound's baritone."

Modestly the cat stretched his neck and gave them a few sample scales, and soon all three were trotting merrily along the road to Bremen.

In a while they approached the outskirts of the city, and came to a farm on the gate of which sat a rooster, crowing as if greeting the dawn.

"What an aria!" exclaimed the donkey. "What operas you could sing, my friend. But tell us, why do you crow so loudly now, when the sun is beginning to set, instead of saving your song for the dawn?"

"It is my last chance," the rooster replied mournfully. "Company is coming for tomorrow's dinner, and the farmer's wife is planning to put me in a soup."

"Dear me!" exclaimed the donkey, "that is the worst yet! Truly, this is a world in which no animal is safe. You had better come along with us, friend rooster, for we are going to Bremen to be town musicians, and it is clear that you have the best voice of us all."

"I will come," said the rooster, hopping down off the gate, and putting both the donkey and the hound between himself and the cat, "for anything would be better than what has been planned for me."

And off they all went down the road as the sun began to set.

"My friends," said the hound, "I am growing footsore, and I cannot see in the dark as some of us can"—here he winked at the cat—"so I would like to suggest that we stop for the night. As you can see, there is a wood on the other side of the road where we may safely conceal ourselves among the trees."

"A fine plan," said the donkey. "We will then arrive in Bremen tomorrow fresh and in good voice."

The cat and the rooster agreed, so the four friends went a little way into the wood and found themselves a large, sheltering tree. The donkey and the hound lay down on either side of the trunk, and the cat and the rooster decided they would be more comfortable in the branches. The cat settled himself halfway up the trunk, but the rooster thought he would be safest at the very top, so up he flew. "I will keep watch," he said, "since I am highest, and I will crow if there is aught amiss."

"Very good, brother," said the donkey, closing his eyes.

"Fine, fine. Good night," said the hound, curling himself into a ball.

"Sleep well, all," said the cat, and commenced to purr.

But the rooster, ever watchful, looked around on all four sides, and when the sky was quite dark, he saw a little light not far in the distance. At the same time it began to rain, so the rooster crowed mightily, waking the others, and said, "Friends, as you see it is raining, but there is a light showing through the trees not far from here. Perhaps it is a house where we might find shelter."

"Good for you," said the cat, shaking rainwater delicately from his paws and climbing backward down the tree trunk. "I say we should make haste."

The dog uncurled from his ball and shook himself. "I agree," he said, shivering—for it was not a warm rain.

The donkey felt the bad weather less than the others, but as he had asked them to throw in their lots with his, he could not very well disagree—and so on they went again.

It did not take them long to arrive at the spot where the light was, and it was indeed coming from a house. The donkey, since he was the tallest, went to the window and, putting his front hooves on the sill, looked in.

"What do you see?" asked the rooster.

"Oh, my!" exclaimed the donkey. "I see a table covered with a cloth, with bread and meat and apples on it, and sitting around the table I see rough men dressed as robbers, and nearby are many great sacks of jewels and gold!"

"The meat sounds good to me," said the hound, licking his chops, "although I never did see much use in gold and jewels."

"Nor did I," said the cat, daintily grooming his whiskers, "but I quite agree about the meat."

"I could reduce that bread to crumbs in no time," said the rooster.

"And there is nothing," said the donkey, "dearer to my heart than a ripe, red, juicy apple. But how are we to get in? And what are we to do with the robbers?"

The animals moved a little way off and discussed what they should do, and at last they thought of a plan. "If we are to be musicians," the donkey said, "this is a fine time to practice!"

So the donkey stood under the window again with his front hooves upon the sill. The hound jumped onto his back, and the cat jumped onto the hound. And the rooster flew up and sat on the cat's head, without hesitation this time, for by now he knew that the cat meant him no harm.

"One—two—three," whispered the donkey, and then they began. The donkey brayed, part bass and part sliding trombone; the hound bayed in his rich baritone, now and then adding percussion in the form of a hearty bark; the cat provided the treble line by singing his tenor air to the moon—and the rooster contributed an operatic aria that would have brought the most critical of audiences to its feet.

And the robbers inside the house leapt up, scattering plates and mugs and what not.

"Heaven help us!" cried their captain, "what is that?"

"It must be the King's Guard," answered one robber in alarm.

"We must flee!" cried another.

And so the robbers burst out the door and fled into the woods.

The four friends, laughing heartily, went inside and fell to with gusto, and for a while there was no sound save their happy munching, gnawing, pecking, and lapping.

"What a concert," said the donkey, when there was nothing left to eat.

"What a meal," said the hound, and then they extinguished the lights and went to bed.

The donkey found some straw in the backyard, and lay down upon it happily; the hound was well pleased to curl up on the back step as he had often done at his master's home; the cat purred by the warm hearth; and the rooster perched upon the roof, hunched his head well down, and soon joined the others in blissful sleep.

When the robbers saw that all was dark and quiet in their house, their courage, such as it was, began to return.

"We were foolish to run," said the captain. "Here—Hans—you go back and see what's what."

Slowly the robber named Hans crept back, keeping to the edges of the yard until he was sure all was still and the house was truly empty. Stealthily, he went in the front door, waking the cat, who opened his eyes. But Hans thought the cat's glowing eyes were two live coals in the fireplace, so be bent down to blow them into flame again—whereupon the cat, whose tail he had stepped on, leapt into his face, spitting and scratching. Hans fled in terror out the back door, tripping over the hound, who bit his

Mayer

leg—and as he ran into the yard he woke the donkey, who kicked him smartly with his hind foot. At that the rooster awoke and began his aria again, the chorus of which was "Cock-a-doodle-do," repeated many times over.

Hans lost no time in running back to the woods. "Oh, captain," he gasped, pale with fright and shaking, "we can never go back again, for our house has been taken over by witches and monsters. Sitting by the hearth is a terrible old witch, who spat at me and scratched my face with nails as sharp, I swear, as a cat's claws! The back door is guarded by a sorcerer with a knife, which he sank into my leg in several places. And in the yard and on the roof are horrible monsters. The one in the yard is huge, with enormous pointed ears; he beat me with a stout club. The one on the roof called out 'That one's a robber, too! You all know what to do!' over and over again."

"Hans," said the robber captain, growing pale, "you have done well. We are clearly lucky to be out of there with our lives. Come, men—we will find ourselves another house."

And so the robbers went far away, to another city in fact, but the Bremen town musicians stayed on, living and singing joyfully till the end of their days. In fact, they became quite famous, as you can tell from this story, which has been told many times in many places.

SNOW WHITE AND ROSE RED

A TIDY cottage stood at the edge of the road to town, but far enough out in the country so there was a wood nearby and a meadow and mountains not far away. In the front yard of the cottage was a pretty garden. Each plant in the garden was more lovely than the next, but loveliest of all were the two rose bushes that peeped in at the cottage's front windows, one with white roses, and the other with red.

In the cottage lived a family of three, a widow and her two daughters, one named Snow White and the other Rose Red, after the flowers from the bushes outside. Snow White was the quieter of the two. In the summer she liked to stay home with her mother, working in the garden and learning to cook and to spin and sew, and reading out of a book of fairy tales that always lay ready near the hearth. Rose Red liked to be more active, running races with the wind that blew across the meadow, and gathering the wild herbs that their mother used in cooking, and chasing butterflies. But every morning, no matter what else they did that day, Snow White brought their mother a white rose from the bush outside the cottage, and Rose Red brought her a red one.

Even though one was quiet and the other was more active, Snow White and Rose Red did most things together, for they were good friends as well as sisters and they enjoyed being with each other. They often went on errands for their mother—gathering berries, collecting firewood, fishing, or even going to town. Their mother never worried about sending them into the wood, for the wild beasts seemed to know and trust them, and protected them from harm. Snow White would often feed cabbage leaves from the garden to the wild hares, and Rose Red would run with the young fawns who chased the sunbeams that filtered through the leaves of the closely growing trees.

Now one summer's day, the two girls wandered farther than usual in the wood, gathering berries, and found they were still far from home when night began to fall. "We must stay here, sister," said Rose Red, "for if we try to find our way in the dark, we will get more lost than we are."

Snow White agreed, so they made themselves a bed of moss and ferns, and lay down, unafraid, to sleep. At dawn when they woke up, Rose Red said, "Look!" to her sister and pointed toward a beautiful child in a shining white robe sitting a little way off from them.

"Good day," called Rose Red.

"Are you lost, too?" asked Snow White.

But the child, though he smiled, never answered. Instead he went away through the trees, and the girls saw that he had been sitting between them and the edge of a high cliff, which they could easily have rolled over in their sleep.

The girls set off through the wood again in the direction the child had gone, and soon found their way home. "That," said their mother when they had told her the story, "must have been an angel, sent by your dear father from heaven to watch over you."

In the winter, the girls had to stay closer to home, for the snow lay deep in the wood and on the road. Rose Red brought in kindling and logs every morning and built up the fire which she had banked the night before, and Snow White fetched water and put the kettle on. Though there were no roses, the girls brought their mother holly with red berries and mistletoe with white berries whenever they could. They spent their days weaving and spinning and baking and polishing and sewing, and tending to all the tasks that could be done better in winter than in summer. In the evenings, Rose Red would bolt the heavy front door and Snow White would fetch the book of fairy tales or another book, and the girls would dream by the fire while their mother read aloud. With them was a lamb that was their pet, and a lovely white dove that perched on the mantel.

One winter night, when the wind was howling and the snow was

swirling in a wild dance, there was a knock at the door. "Open the door, Rose Red," said the girls' mother, "for whoever it is must be perishing with cold."

So Rose Red got up from the fire and ran to the door, drawing back the bolt and letting in a great blast of wind and snow. Before her mother and sister could see what was there, they heard her scream. The lamb bleated in alarm and ran away, and the dove flew from her perch up into the rafters high under the cottage roof. Then Snow White saw that a great black bear had come in, and she hid behind her mother, trembling.

The bear shook some of the snow off himself and spoke. "Do not be afraid," he said. "I will not harm anyone here; I swear it. I mean no one any harm; I am simply seeking shelter from the storm. May I warm myself awhile by your fire?"

The girls' mother was the first to recover from her fright, and she, seeing that the bear seemed in all ways gentle, said, "Poor, poor bear, you do indeed look frozen! Of course come to the fire and lie down on the hearth. Come, girls," she said, when the bear gratefully settled himself in the warmth. "Do not hide; he is a gentle beast, like your friends in the forest." So Snow White and Rose Red crept closer, but they were still wary until the lamb came out of hiding and curled up next to the bear, and the dove flew back to her perch on the mantel.

"Children," said the bear, "there is still snow on my coat, and it is making puddles on the floor. Would you brush it out for me?"

The girls' mother brought the broom and a little pan, and Snow White and Rose Red took turns sweeping the snow from the bear's coat. Rose Red swept quickly and vigorously, but on her own turn, Snow White thought she saw something glitter in the bear's fur. Since she was not sure, she said nothing about it.

When the bear's coat was free of snow, he grunted happily and stretched himself out, and was dozing by the time the girls and their mother went to bed. The next morning he was still there, but asked to be let out, and the children found they were sorry to see him go. Happily that night there was again a knocking at the door and he was there once more. Soon the friendly black bear came every night to sleep beside the fire, and each night before he slept he let the girls play with him. He gave Snow White rides on his back and let Rose Red wrestle with him, and he was in all ways as gentle and as friendly as a large, floppy dog. Still once in a while Snow White thought she saw something glitter and shine in his coat, but whenever she looked for it, it was gone, and so she said nothing of it.

The winter months passed happily in this way. In time, the air softened and the snow melted and the earliest flowers began springing up in the garden outside the cottage. Soon the buds on the trees and on the rose bushes swelled and then before the leaves were well out, the bear said, "Now my friends, I must leave you and go back to my home for the summer. But I thank you for your kindness."

"Where is your home?" cried Snow White, "for I will miss you terribly! Perhaps we could come and see you."

"My home is in the deep forest beyond your little wood," said the bear, "a long way from here and across a river. I have to go back to keep my treasure safe from the dwarfs, who will steal it if I am not there to guard its hiding place. In the winter when the ground is frozen they cannot come up from their underground caves, but when the ground thaws, they can, and if they find what I have, they will take it from me. They have already taken some."

"But what do you have?" asked Rose Red, thinking that a bear's treasure would be honey and berries and other food not interesting to dwarfs, who she had read liked gold and silver and precious stones.

But at this the bear only smiled and said again that he must leave. When he did, Snow White again thought she saw something glitter and shine under his coat, but she was not sure and so said nothing of it.

Not long after that, because there were still chilly days and cold nights, the girls' mother asked them to go out to collect firewood. There were always dead trees lying on the ground that the girls could strip of branches, cut into logs, and carry home. They had not been looking long before they saw a large tree on the ground and, after discussing it, were about to turn away, for it seemed too big for them to handle safely. Suddenly Rose Red cried, "Look, Snow White, something is moving there—maybe some animal is making a nest or a den under the tree!"

The girls crept to the tree on tiptoe, not wanting to frighten whatever animal was there—although it seemed already frightened, for it was frantically jumping up and down.

"Perhaps it has caught its tail," whispered Snow White—and then she put her hand on her sister's arm, stopping her, and drew in her breath.

There was no need for Snow White to say what she saw, for Rose Red saw it at the same time: a dwarf with a white beard as long as he was tall, and a face so wrinkled that he must have been at least one hundred years old. The dwarf's beard was caught in a place where the tree was partly split, which was why he was jumping up and down.

As the girls stood there wondering what to do, he saw them and said angrily, "Has no one told you it is rude to stare? Can you not make yourselves useful instead of gawking like a couple of crude market women?"

"You poor thing," said Rose Red. "How can we help you?"

"You can help me free my beard, you stupid salamander; what does it look as if you can do? There I was, ready to split this tree into logs for firewood, and my wedge slipped out of the cut I had made and my beard slipped in and the wood closed upon it. Well, come along, stop staring and start doing!"

Rose Red did not think it would be polite to tell the dwarf that most people cut trees into logs *before* they split them, and that in any case, this tree was far too big for so small a creature as he—for indeed, he was even smaller than the two girls.

"Come, sister," said Snow White, going to the little man and laying hold of his beard, "let us see if we can pull it out."

"Ow! Ow! Ow!" cried the dwarf, as the two children tugged with all their might. "More gently, you great, rough creatures!"

"Perhaps," said Rose Red, "you could hold your beard steady above where we are pulling—so—and it will not hurt you so much."

"And," said Snow White, "perhaps if you do not jump back as we pull, it will not hurt you at all."

"Harumph!" said the unpleasant little dwarf, but he did as the girls suggested and this time, though he was not hurt, the beard did not come out one bit.

"Where are your wedges?" asked Rose Red. "Perhaps we can drive them in a little way, and make the cut larger."

"You foolish girl," said the dwarf. "And have them spring out again and catch me on the head?"

"Well," said Snow White, "perhaps if you will not accept help from us, you will from someone else. There is a woodcutter's cottage not far from here. . . ."

"You are even stupider than your sister," said the ill-tempered little creature. "Would you leave me here to be devoured by the wild beasts? There are"—he shuddered—"bears in this forest."

The girls exchanged a look and they said, "Yes, we know," but Snow White almost giggled out loud at the thought of their kindly black bear devouring anyone.

"Now," said Rose Red, "let us have one more try," and she seized the beard again.

"You did that already," cried the dwarf, stamping his foot. "Can you not think of anything else?"

"Yes," said Snow White, who had had enough. She took her scissors from her apron pocket and held them up to Rose Red where the dwarf could not see. Rose Red nodded, and without another word, Snow White snipped off the very end of the dwarf's beard, freeing it instantly.

"Now look what you have done!" cried the dwarf in a rage, reaching for a bag that he had hidden under the tree; there was gold in it. "You have cut off the best part of my fine, white beard! It will take many weeks for it to grow back again!" And without even a word of thanks, he shouldered his bag of gold and hopped off.

"What a nasty creature," said Rose Red, when he was gone.

"Horrible," agreed Snow White, "but he did look funny, jumping up and down." And the two girls giggled about that for the rest of the day.

A few weeks later, when the weather was so much warmer there was rarely a need for a fire except for cooking, Snow White and Rose Red went to the river to catch fish for dinner. It was one of the things they liked best to do, for they could drop their lines in the water and then sit on the bank of the river and tell stories, which is what Snow White liked best and then, when they tired of that, it was Rose Red's turn. They would prop their rods up with stones and play tag among the cat-o'-nine-tails until one of them saw the tip of a rod move and cried, "Look—a bite!"

On this day when they reached the river they saw something jumping up and down at its edge. "Now what do you suppose that is?" said Snow White. "An otter, do you think, playing there, or a beaver working?"

"No," cried Rose Red, running ahead, "it is neither—it is our old friend the dwarf!"

"Friend, indeed," said Snow White. "Come—let us go further down the bank; he is nothing but trouble."

"I am afraid that he is *in* trouble," said Rose Red. "Look—his beard seems caught again, in his fishing line this time. What a stupid dwarf he is!"

"What, me stupid?" cried the dwarf, who had overheard them. "Come closer and you will see it is not my doing at all, but a terrible fish who is doing his best to pull me into the water. It is the wind's fault for wrapping my beard around the fishing line just as this big fellow struck—oh, help, help, before he pulls me in and I drown!"

So Rose Red put her arms around the dwarf and Snow White put her arms around Rose Red and they tugged against the fish but it did no good.

"Sir dwarf," said Rose Red at last, gasping for breath, "I am very sorry but I do not think we can keep you from the water much longer. Perhaps if my sister has her scissors with her, she can again cut your beard."

"What," cried the dwarf, "are you barbers, then, you two, that you would do nothing but cut hair? You wish to make me ugly!"

At this it was all the girls could do to keep from laughing, for indeed the dwarf was already as ugly as anything could be. But then the fish gave a great tug and even the dwarf could see that there was no other solution. So while Rose Red kept on pulling with the dwarf against the fish, Snow White took out her scissors and snipped away at the beard till at last the tangled part was freed, and Rose Red and the dwarf fell over in a heap.

"You miserable mushrooms," cried the dwarf, jumping to his feet and picking up another bag, this one full of pearls, which he had hidden in the tall grass beside the river. "Again you disfigure me! It will now be months before my beautiful beard grows back; until it does, I will have to remain in hiding or be laughed at." And off he went, with never so much as a thank-you, his bag of pearls over his shoulder.

"He still has plenty of beard left," said Snow White, as Rose Red got to her feet and brushed herself off. "Are you all right?"

"Yes," said Rose Red, "and you are right about his beard—although I think we may one day wish you had cut off the whole thing, since he is forever getting it tangled."

After that, the two girls gradually settled down to their fishing, and by evening they had each caught a fine trout, which their mother rolled in oats and then fried.

Not long afterward, during high summer, when the wheat and corn were tall and thick in the fields and bees buzzed contentedly in the sweet clover, the girls' mother sent them to town to buy thread and ribbons and laces and needles and pins. "For," she said, "we must always think of the winter that lies ahead, and make sure we have enough put by."

So the girls set out early one morning, before the sun grew too hot.

The road passed along the edge of the wood and soon came into open country, where there was a long, barren stretch with many rocks and next to no grass. As the girls came to this place, they saw an eagle circling low in the sky, as if hunting. As they came closer, they saw the bird drop suddenly toward the ground, and a moment later, they heard a scream.

They ran to the place and were horrified to see the very same dwarf as before, dangling from the eagle's talons.

The sight was so horrible that Snow White and Rose Red forgot all else and set about to free the dwarf. They ran to him and, reaching up, grasped him around the legs and pulled. Although they could not at first free him, they succeeded in stopping the eagle in mid-flight, so that he had to hang suspended in the air, so heavy was his burden now that the two girls had added their weight to the dwarf's. At last the eagle grew tired, and the girls, seeing that he flagged, gave one mighty pull, and the eagle dropped his burden and soared off angrily into the sky.

"No-good nanny-goats!" cried the dwarf. "Nincompoops! Clumsy oafs! Did you have to be so rough? Did you have to twist and turn while hanging onto my legs with your great weight? My muscles will be cramped for many a day because of you two." And with that, again without even a hint of thanks, the dwarf picked up a bag of precious stones that had been lying nearby and vanished into a hole under one of the largest rocks.

"I never," said Snow White. "He should win a prize for rudeness. But I suppose it is his way."

"Let us hope it is a way we will meet no more," said Rose Red, and so the girls continued on their way to the town, where they bought the thread and ribbons and laces and needles and pins for their mother, and then they set out on their way home again.

They reached the barren place as the sun was beginning to set, and who should they see but the dwarf again. He had emptied his bag of precious stones out onto a flat rock, along with his bag of gold and his bag of pearls, and was counting his riches. The sun caught in the cut edges of the stones and glinted off them; its rays made the pearls glow softly with iridescent whiteness, and made the gold shine as if it held the sun's light inside it. The girls were overwhelmed and stood staring.

"You again!" snarled the dwarf when he saw them. "Why do you stand and stare? That is all you ever do—stare at misfortune, stare at jewels. Now—now—now where was I?" he sputtered. "You have made me lose count, you wretched rabbits, and I shall have to start again." He was so angry his face became quite red, and he stepped with menace toward the girls, who found themselves truly afraid of him for the first time since they had encountered him by the fallen tree.

Just as they were most afraid, they heard a growling sound, and there lumbering out of the wood came a large black bear. The bear leapt angrily at the dwarf and said, "I have you now, you wicked thing, in the act of counting what is not yours." And the bear chased the dwarf across the barren field. The dwarf could not escape him, and soon was caught.

"Oh, good sir bear," begged the dwarf, whining, "please spare my miserable life and I will give you all these treasures in return—my gold, my pearls, and my precious stones; see how they all glimmer in the setting sun. And to add to your pleasure, you may take these two rosy girls, who, though stupid and tiresome, are quite plump and no doubt succulent; they would make a fine dinner for you, I'll warrant."

At this the bear's roars became terrifying and with his paw he smote the dwarf such a heavy blow that the dwarf was still, and moved no more.

Snow White and Rose Red had hidden behind a large boulder during this terrifying scene and were still cowering there when it was over and all was quiet once more. But then they heard a familiar voice, growly but soft and full of fondness, and it was the bear's voice. "Snow White, Rose Red," it said, "my little friends, it is I, your friend of the winter! Do not be afraid but come out and play with me once again." And at that the girls came out of hiding and recognized their own bear and smiled at him and embraced him. And when their gentle hands caressed his head, the bearskin that covered him fell off and there stood before them a handsome young man, dressed in a suit of gold. Snow White gasped, remembering how often she had seen something shining beneath the bear's furry coat.

The young man bowed low before the two girls and said, "I am a prince, son of the king of the kingdom across the river, and I was turned into a bear by that very same dwarf. He stole the gold and the pearls and the precious stones from me and when I tried to get them back he enchanted me. I have had to live as a bear till his death, guarding my remaining riches as best I could. But now I am free again, and can claim my lost treasures. And someday, I hope, also my bride," he said, smiling at Snow White.

So the prince gathered up his treasures and he and the two girls went merrily home to the cottage by the road. On the way the prince told them that he had a brother, who still lived in the kingdom across the river, and who was young and as handsome as he, but had never married. In time it fell out that Snow White married this selfsame prince who had been the bear, and Rose Red married his brother, and the girls' mother went to live with them in the palace. But she soon missed her little cottage and her garden and her rose bushes and the pet lamb and the dove. So the two princes had the cottage brought to the palace grounds, along with the lamb and the dove, and they had all the plants in the garden dug up and moved also, flower by flower and bush by bush. Now the old mother lives there happily with the lamb and the dove, and every morning her daughters, the princesses Snow White and Rose Red, wake her by bringing her one white rose and one red rose from the same bush that grew outside their cottage windows when they were children. They are all most content and happy, and love each other well.

FUNDEVOGEL

ONCE when a certain forester was out hunting, he heard a sound as if a baby were crying. He was a tenderhearted man, and followed the sound until he came to a tall tree. Much to his astonishment, he saw a small child at the top of it, in a bird's nest.

The forester climbed up and the child put his arms out eagerly to be saved. "How did you get here, little one?" the forester asked, tying the child to his back and climbing down with him.

"A terrible bird took me from my mother," the little boy said, "and I do not know where she is now." He began to cry.

"There, there, little one," said the forester, comforting him. "I will call you Fundevogel, for that means bird-that-was-found, and indeed you *were* very like a little bird, sitting high up in that nest. I will take you home with me, and if we cannot find your mother, you will be my son, and brother to my little daughter Lina."

So the forester took Fundevogel home, and looked far and wide for his mother. He never found her, though, so Fundevogel and Lina became like brother and sister, and were very happy together. In fact, they grew to love each other so much that where one went, the other always followed, and when they had to be away from each other only for a minute, they were broken-hearted.

Now the forester's wife was dead, so the children had no mother to love and care for them. The forester was rich enough to have servants, and chief among them was a woman named Sanna, who worked as cook and housekeeper; it was Sanna who had charge of the children. But Sanna was really a witch, and though she hid it from the forester, she did not like

Fundevogel, nor did she know how fond Lina and Fundevogel were of each other.

One evening, Lina saw Sanna making trip after trip to the spring, filling many buckets with water and pouring the water into her big iron pot. "Sanna," she asked, "why do you need so much water? Is company coming, or are you going to wash all our clothes at once?"

"Hush," said Sanna. Then she said, "I can only tell you if you will never tell anyone else."

"I never will," said Lina. "Please tell me."

"Very early tomorrow morning," said Sanna, "when your father is out hunting, I will light a fire under my big iron pot, and when it is boiling merrily, I will throw Fundevogel in."

Lina was horrified, but, though she no longer felt bound by her promise not to tell, for the moment she just nodded at Sanna, and kept silent for the rest of the evening. But the next morning, when the forester had left to look after some newly planted trees and Sanna had gone outside to light her fire, Lina said to Fundevogel, "If you will never leave me, little brother, I will never leave you."

"I will never leave you," answered Fundevogel, "not now, or ever."

"Fundevogel, we must run away," said Lina, and she told him what Sanna had said to her.

So the two children tiptoed out of the house, and went deep into the forest.

In a while the water boiled, and Sanna went to find Fundevogel and throw him in. But the children were nowhere to be found, and she grew alarmed and said, "What shall I tell the forester when he comes home and finds both children gone?" She had planned to tell him that Fundevogel's mother had returned for him—but what could she tell him about Lina? "Fundevogel's being gone would be one thing," she said to herself, "but Lina—that is quite another!" So she ordered three servants to go out and look for the children.

The servants followed the path the children had taken into the forest, and soon Lina saw them drawing near. So she said to Fundevogel, "If you will never leave me, little brother, I will never leave you."

And Fundevogel answered, "I will never leave you. Not now, or ever."

"Fundevogel," said Lina, "the servants are coming after us; turn yourself into a rose tree, and I will become a rose on one of your branches."

In a few minutes the servants came to where the children had been, but all they found was a rose tree with a single rose flowering upon it, so they went on. And later, when they went back to Sanna, they told her they had found nothing except a rose tree with one rose.

"Fools!" cried the witch-cook. "Do you not know that rose trees do not grow in forests? You should have cut it down and brought me the rose; go back and do it at once."

The servants ran back into the forest, but Lina saw them coming and said, "Fundevogel, if you will never leave me, I will never leave you."

Fundevogel answered, "I will never leave you, Lina. Not now, or ever."

"They are coming for us again," she told him, "so you must become a church, and I will be a chandelier hanging from your rafters."

In a minute the servants arrived, and ran inside the church and looked for the children behind all its pews and up and down the stairs and even in the high steeple, but they found nothing and so they went on. And later, when they got back to the forester's house, they told Sanna they had found nothing in the woods but a church with a beautiful chandelier hanging in it.

"Fools," said Sanna, "do you not know there was never a church in those woods before? You must go back and tear it down, and bring me the chandelier."

This time the old witch-cook followed along behind them.

The children saw the servants coming, and saw Sanna running after them, huffing and puffing. "Fundevogel," said Lina, "never leave me, and I will never leave you."

"I will never leave you, Lina," said Fundevogel, "not now, or ever."

"Become a fishpond," said Lina quickly, "for as you see Sanna is coming with them this time—and I will be a duck swimming on the pond."

And so instead of a church, the servants and Sanna found a pond and a duck, and the servants, bewildered, started looking among the rushes and lilypads, but Sanna threw herself down on her stomach, and opened her mouth to drink the pond up. But Lina, in duck-shape, swam up to her, seized her hair in her beak, and pulled the witch into the water, where she drowned.

And then the two children turned back into themselves, and went home merrily. As far as anyone knows, they are together still.

RAPUNZEL

ONCE upon a time there was a good woman who lived with her husband in a humble house next to a beautiful walled garden. "How lucky we are," the woman often said to her husband, "that we can see into that lovely garden from our upstairs window—for no one, it seems, is allowed inside."

For years the woman was content to look at the garden from a distance. Eagerly she watched its flowers and herbs progress from spring buds to summer flowers to autumn seeds, and she waited impatiently through winter's cold for the snow to melt and for spring to come again. But then there came a year when the woman was expecting a child, and as spring turned to summer, she found she was no longer content with just looking. One whole garden bed this year had been planted with rampion, a bellflower with a delicious root like a white radish, and when the woman noticed how lush and crisp the rampion plants were, her mouth began to water, and she felt she must have some or die. Day after day she stood silently at the upstairs window, staring out at the rampion, till her husband could bear it no longer.

"What is it, my dear?" he asked one morning. "What is wrong?"

"Oh, husband," the woman answered, "see how green the leaves of that rampion are! Can you not imagine the delectable roots? Do you not long for a salad—a fresh rampion salad, crisp and cool? I feel I must have some of that rampion or die." And she sank down weakly onto a chair—for, indeed, she had been able to eat little ordinary food at all, so consumed was she with longing for the rampion.

Now the husband dearly loved his wife, and he paled to hear her say she must have some of the rampion or die. So that very evening when the sun had set, he dropped a rope over the garden wall from the upstairs window of his house, and carefully let himself down. His heart beat wildly in fear lest he be caught by whoever owned the garden, but he made his way quickly to the rampion bed, pulled up two big bunches of the most luxuriant plants, and hastily climbed back up to his wife, the rampion fastened under his belt.

Though it was full night by then, the woman immediately made a huge salad and fell to with such gusto that the husband laughed with joy to see her happy at last. "Delicious," she said, "oh, splendid—oh, it is so good! Will you not have some, too?"

"No, my dear," he said, shaking his head. "It is enough to see you enjoy yourself so thoroughly." And they went to bed happily for the first time in many weeks.

But by afternoon of the very next day, the wife was at the window again, staring out at the garden and sighing.

"Alas, wife," her husband said, "what is it now?"

"Oh, husband," she answered sadly, "that rampion was so good—so succulent, so pungently delicious—that I cannot rest until I have some more." And she sank down into her chair again, seeming to grow pale before his eyes.

So that evening, too, once it was dark, the husband let himself down into the garden on his rope—but this time as his feet touched the ground, a cold hand gripped his shoulder and an icy voice said, "So—it is you who steals my rampion!"

The husband, his heart now beating even more wildly than before, looked at his captor and trembled, for her face was harsh and stern. "Forgive me, madam," he murmured, "but my wife, who will soon bear our child, longs so for your delicious rampion I fear she will die if I deny it her."

"Very well," said the witch—for though she was known in the village harmlessly as Dame Gothel, witch she was—"you may have all the rampion you want for your wife, but I will have something in return."

"Anything, anything," the man promised eagerly. "Oh, anything at all!"

"I will have your child," said the witch, "the moment it is born. Do not fear—I will look after it well, as tenderly as a mother. But I have no child of my own, and I long for one."

Now the husband wanted to protest. How could he give up his own child and how could he ask that of his wife? But Dame Gothel fixed him with her witch's eyes, and he knew instantly that it would be impossible to refuse.

Time passed, and the wife had all the rampion she wanted, but when at the end of the summer she gave birth to a beautiful baby girl, Dame Gothel appeared in her room, and took the child away.

The witch named the baby Rapunzel, which is another word for rampion. She cared for her kindly, although she did not let her play with other children, or see any other person save herself. Rapunzel grew to be more beautiful than any other girl had ever been, and when she was twelve years old, the witch took her to a tall tower with no stairs and no doors. She shut Rapunzel up in its very top, where light came in through only a single, small window. Whenever Dame Gothel wished to visit her, or take her food, she would stand at the foot of the tower and say:

Rapunzel fair,
Let down your hair.

Rapunzel would then unbraid her lovely golden hair and let it down, first fastening it to some hooks that were under the window. Dame Gothel then climbed up, using Rapunzel's hair as a rope, and it did not hurt Rapunzel, for the hooks kept it from pulling.

Time passed slowly for Rapunzel high in her tower. She did have a few books, and once in a while Dame Gothel brought her some sewing to do, but, except for Dame Gothel, who came every other evening, she had no one to talk to save the birds that occasionally lighted on the window-sill. To amuse herself, Rapunzel often made up songs—for she knew no written ones, since she had been cut off from the world. Whenever she sang, her clear voice soared out over the lonely forest from the high tower, and all the woodland creatures stopped whatever they were doing to listen.

One day, after a few years had passed and Rapunzel was nearly grown up, a prince rode through the forest and stopped his horse in amazement when he heard Rapunzel's lovely voice. Following the sound, he soon came to the high tower, and he stood up in his stirrups and called, "Hello! Lady in the tower!"

But Rapunzel, who was still singing, could not hear him, and he rode sadly away. "But," he reasoned, "she must come out of the tower sometimes, or someone must go in to her; I have only to watch and I am bound to learn if she is as beautiful as her voice."

So the prince went back to the tower, and hid his horse, and took cover under some nearby bushes to wait.

Soon Dame Gothel appeared, a basket of food on her arm. She stood beneath the tower and called:

Rapunzel fair,
Let down your hair.

First the witch attached the food basket to Rapunzel's hair, and when Rapunzel appeared in the window, pulling it up, the prince gasped to see how beautiful she was. Then as the witch climbed up herself, he thought, If the only way into that tower is the lady's hair, she must be prisoner there. Perhaps she will let me climb up and save her.

So the next evening, the brave prince, after first making sure Dame Gothel was not in sight, stood under the tower and, disguising his voice, called:

Rapunzel fair,
Let down your hair.

Down came the golden cascade, and up he climbed.

"Oh!" Rapunzel cried, shrinking from the prince in fright when he appeared in the window. "Where is Dame Gothel? And who are you—what are you?"—for Rapunzel had never seen a man before.

"I am a prince," the man replied gently, "and I mean you no harm. Your singing was so beautiful I felt I must see if the owner of the voice was as lovely as her songs. Now I find that she is more so." The prince talked to Rapunzel quietly for some time, sitting on the windowsill, and at last she let him inside the tower, and told him her story.

And so it happened that the prince visited Rapunzel every other evening, when Dame Gothel did not come. He told her of the wonders of the world, and grew to love her, and she him. One night when the stars and moon were bright and the air was soft with early summer, he took her hand and said, "My dearest Rapunzel, I love you more than life itself, and you love me. Will you be my wife? Will you let me take you from this tower so that we can be together forever?"

"Oh, yes," Rapunzel answered. "Oh, yes! But how am I to get down from the tower? I cannot climb down my own hair."

"No," said the prince, "but you could climb down a ladder."

"What is a ladder?" Rapunzel asked, and when the prince had explained, she shook her head and said, "No—for what if Dame Gothel—or anyone else—saw you carrying it here? Or what if she passed by and saw it? And afterward—what would we do with it? It sounds too large a thing to hide."

The two fell silent for a time, discouraged, and then at last Rapunzel said, "I know! Each time you come, bring me some silk, and I will twine it into a ladder, but it will be so light and thin I will be able to hide it, and we will be able to take it with us easily when we leave. No one will see you carrying anything at all."

So every other evening the prince brought Rapunzel some silk, and every other day she twined it with the silk he had already brought, slowly fashioning a strong but delicate ladder, which she hid easily in her bed.

Then late one night Rapunzel fell ill with a fever, and by the next evening she was so sick she did not remember whose turn it was to visit her, the prince's or Dame Gothel's. She thought, however, that it was the prince's turn, and felt, as her visitor climbed up, that it must indeed be he from the way her hair twisted below the hooks, as if the climber was eager to arrive. So she was glad and greeted the prince by name—but, alas, it was the witch instead, who cried angrily, "That is not my name—you wicked girl, you have betrayed me!" Dame Gothel flung about the room, searching for she knew not what, till she found the half-made ladder and knew from it that Rapunzel planned to escape. "I will put you where no one will find you," she cried, shredding the ladder to bits with the scissors she always kept with her. Then she cut off Rapunzel's beautiful hair. "This is for your wickedness," she said, "and for my revenge." Poor Rapunzel wept bitterly, but the witch paid her no heed, and transported her to a desert, separated from the world she knew by miles and miles of empty sand.

Then the witch returned to the tower and attached Rapunzel's hair to the hooks under the window. The next evening when the prince came and called softly:

Rapunzel fair,
Let down your hair,

the witch let fall the hair she had cut from Rapunzel's head, and hid as the prince climbed in through the window. Then, triumphantly, she showed herself, and said, "Your little singing bird has escaped, evil one, but see how the cat awaits you." And she scratched at him and fought with him till he fell from the tower into some thorns, which scratched his eyes and made him blind.

For a long time the prince wandered sadly through the world, searching for Rapunzel as best he could, though he had no sight. Everywhere he went he cried:

Rapunzel fair,
Let down your hair!
I cannot see—
Please sing to me.

But there was seldom an answering voice, and when there was, it was never the right one.

Then one day after years had passed, the prince stumbled onto the hot sand of the desert and decided to walk on, thinking, If a witch were to hide someone from the world, she might well hide her in a desert into which no one ventures. So on he walked, across miles of wasteland, crying:

Rapunzel fair,
Let down your hair!
I cannot see—
Please sing to me.

And after two days, so faintly at first he could scarcely hear it, came an answering voice—a voice of such beauty that he knew it to be Rapunzel's. Besides, she sang the song he had first heard long ago from the tower and had never forgotten. He followed the sound as he had done before, and soon came to the place where she was, and they embraced joyfully. Rapunzel wept for his blindness, and her tears fell on his eyes and healed them. Then they returned to the prince's kingdom, and his father the king caught and punished the witch. He brought Rapunzel's parents to the palace when Rapunzel and the prince were married. In time they themselves were the parents of twins, a boy and a girl, and they all lived happily together for many years to come.

HANSEL AND GRETEL

IN a thick, deep forest not far from a lake, there once lived a poor woodcutter and his two children—Hansel and his younger sister, Gretel. The children's mother was dead and the woodcutter had gotten married again—to a selfish woman who did not like children. The family was poor day in and day out, and when hard times came and even the rich had little to spare, they had next to nothing at all. "How," the woodcutter wondered aloud one night after the children were in bed, "are we to go on? How am I to feed us now?"

"I will tell you how," said the selfish stepmother. "We will turn the children out on their own, and then we will have what little there is for ourselves."

"No, no," the woodcutter cried, horrified, "we can never do that!"

But as time went on, there was less and less food to be had, and fewer and fewer people bought or traded for the woodcutter's wood. The selfish woman finally said, "Husband, the children will manage. We will take them halfway through the woods, and we will build a fire for them, and we will give them some bread. They will not find their way home, but someone else—some hunter, perhaps—is sure to take them in."

"No," said the man, "the wild animals will eat them. Hush!"

"They will not," said his wife. "The fire will keep the animals away." She went to the cupboard and threw it open, showing him that there was barely food there for two, let alone for four. "If we do not do this, husband," the selfish woman said, "we will *all* starve. This way, we will all have a chance. Who knows," she said, "perhaps they will be better off than us in the end." She went on and on in this vein, till the poor woodcutter had no peace, so at last, unhappily, he gave in.

But on the night when the parents made their final plans, the children were unable to sleep because of the hunger that gnawed at their empty stomachs. "What shall we do?" Gretel said, weeping. "How will we manage all alone in the forest?"

"Hush, Gretel," Hansel said, trying to comfort her. "We will find some way; hush, and let me think."

Hansel waited till the woodcutter and his wife were asleep and then he went outside and filled his pockets with the white pebbles that lay about the cottage. The moon made the pebbles shine as bright as pennies, and Hansel smiled as he picked them up, and slept contentedly when he went back inside again.

In the morning, the selfish stepmother shook the children awake. "Up, up, up!" she scolded. "Up, lazybones, up! You must come to the forest to help us gather wood." She handed them each a small piece of bread, saying, "Save this for your dinner, for there is no more; this will be your only meal today." And off they all went into the forest, Hansel with his pockets filled with pebbles, and Gretel with the bread under her apron.

As they walked, Hansel turned every now and then, pretending to look behind but in truth dropping pebbles in the path. "Hansel," said the woodcutter at last, "hurry up, boy—you are lagging. Why do you keep looking back?"

"I'm looking at a cat, Father, who is sunning itself behind us."

The stepmother turned back then and said, "That is no cat, you foolish boy; it is just the sun shining on the lake."

At last they came to the middle of the forest, and the father began cutting wood, leaving aside some of the best pieces. "Gather kindling, children," he said sadly, "for we will soon build a fire to keep you warm." When there was a big pile of kindling, the woodcutter laid logs on top of it, and lit it. "Lie down by the fire, children," said the stepmother. "You may have your dinner and a nap while your father and I go further into the forest and cut more wood. We will be back by evening."

The children sat down by the fire, and after a time ate their bread, and then fell asleep. "Perhaps they are not going to leave us after all," said Gretel when they woke near nightfall—for they could both hear the thwack! thwack! of their father's axe upon the trees.

But the night deepened, and the parents did not come back. Hansel moved a little distance from the fire and found a branch which the stepmother had fastened to a tree in such a way that it would blow back and forth in the wind, making the children think their father was nearby. "They are not coming back, Gretel," he said, and Gretel began to cry.

"Don't cry, little sister," Hansel said. "We will be fine when the moon rises; just wait and see."

In a while, the moon did rise, full and splendid, and it shone on the white pebbles Hansel had dropped, and made them glimmer again like bright, new pennies.

Hansel took his little sister's hand, and for the rest of the night they followed the pebbles, until at dawn they came to their own cottage again.

"You bad children!" the stepmother scolded as if they had done something wrong. "Why did you stray from the fire? We thought you would never find your way."

But the woodcutter put his arms around his children without saying a word, and hugged them close.

As it happened, the woodcutter and his wife had managed to get a good price for the wood they had cut that day, and so had been able to buy flour for bread, and a few potatoes and onions, and even some nuts and one or two large apples. For a while, the family had enough to eat again.

But then fierce storms destroyed the crops for miles around, and there were many more people than there was work to be done, and times were bad again. Once more the woodcutter and his family had even less than other people, and again the selfish stepmother began talking of abandoning the children. "We have next to nothing now," Hansel and Gretel heard her say one night, "and after this last loaf of bread is gone, there will be nothing at all—and no chance of buying flour this time even if someone did want our wood, for there is no longer any wheat for the miller to grind into flour. If the children were gone, perhaps we could live on the bread we have until we find something else."

"It would be better," said the woodcutter, "to share our last meal with the children than to send them away."

But his wife would hear none of that. On and on she talked until again the poor woodcutter, weeping, agreed—but he hoped in his heart that the children might find their way to a kinder mother.

"We will take them further this time," the stepmother said, "and we will make sure they have no means of marking the way back." So saying, she locked the door, put the key in her pocket, and went to bed.

"Oh, Hansel, what shall we do?" wept Gretel, when their parents were asleep. "Now you cannot even go outside and get pebbles. How will we ever find our way home?"

"Don't cry, Gretel," Hansel said—but he was worried himself, nonetheless. "We will think of something—perhaps someone will find us this time, or we will find someone." But this time Hansel did not sleep.

"Up, up, up, lazybones!" cried the selfish stepmother at dawn. When the children were dressed, she gave them each a morsel of bread, smaller than before. Gretel put hers under her apron, but Hansel kept his in his hand, and as they walked through the forest, he stopped every so often, breaking off a crumb and dropping it on the ground. "Hansel," said the woodcutter, "why do you keep turning around?"

"There is a pigeon behind us, Father," he said. "I am watching it."

"Foolish boy!" said the stepmother crossly. "That is not a pigeon; it is the sun sparkling on the dew that fell in the night."

But Hansel ignored her, and went on breaking off tiny crumbs and throwing them down.

Soon the woodcutter wanted to stop, but the stepmother led them all on further, till they reached a spot more than halfway through the forest, where they had never been before. Again the father cut logs and the children were set to gather kindling, and soon there was enough wood for a fire. "Rest here, children," said the stepmother, when the fire was burning brightly, "and we will be back for you by nightfall. Do not stray this time as you did before," she added.

"It will be all right, Gretel," Hansel whispered, "even if they do not come back—you will see." He told her about the bread he had dropped.

At dinnertime, Gretel shared her bread with Hansel, and then they fell asleep till nightfall. "Hansel," Gretel cried, when they woke, "I do not see the crumbs you dropped!"

"Never fear, Gretel," he said. "When the moon rises you will see them."

But he was wrong, for birds had eaten the crumbs almost as fast as he had dropped them, and there were none left.

"Never mind," Hansel said, "we will still find the way. See—we came from over there, I think, past that large oak tree, and around that pine."

But, though both Hansel and Gretel kept seeing trees and rocks and bushes that looked like those they had seen before, they were soon lost and walking in circles as lost people often do. They walked all night without finding their way, and they walked all the next day as well, and had only a few berries to eat which they found growing along the way.

On the second night, they slept, for they were too weary to walk farther, and then started out again at dawn the next day. But they walked more slowly now, for they were so tired and hungry that it was almost impossible for them to put one foot ahead of the other.

At noontime on the third day, Gretel suddenly pointed to a beautiful white bird sitting above them in a tree. The bird sang so prettily that they both stood still to listen. Soon the bird stretched its wings and flew, dipping down close to them, flying ahead and then coming back, as if it wanted them to follow.

"Maybe it will lead us out of the forest," said Hansel, so they ran after the bird.

The bird led them not out of the forest but to a little house, where it perched for a moment before flying away again.

"Mmmm," Hansel said hungrily, "someone must be baking—I smell bread!"

Gretel reached up to knock on the door, then squealed in surprise. "Hansel, look!" she cried; "the door is covered with gingerbread—no, the door *is* gingerbread." She broke off a bit of molding and ate it hungrily.

"And the walls," cried Hansel, full of wonder and delight. "Why, the walls are made of bread." He, too, began breaking off pieces—small ones at first and then larger. "And the windows are made of sugar—the panes are clear sugar, not glass," he said.

"And the windowsills are cakes," said Gretel happily, "and so are the slates on the roof. . . ."

Hansel reached up to the low roof, and broke off a piece for himself and one for Gretel, and then Gretel began to eat a small window.

Nibble, nibble, like a mouse—
Who is eating up my house?

The children froze, hearing those words coming softly from inside. But then they answered:

The wind, the wind,
Hear how it blows!

They made wind noises and then, when the voice from inside fell silent, they went on eating: Hansel had a larger slate, and Gretel pushed out an entire windowpane, from a large window this time.

Then the voice came again:

Nibble, nibble, like a mouse—
Who is eating up my house?

And with that the gingerbread door opened, and an old, stooped woman made her way slowly out, groping because she could not see very well. Hansel and Gretel were both terrified, and dropped what they were eating. But the woman smiled and said, "Poor, hungry children, do not be afraid. Come in, come in, and I will give you better food." The children were so hungry that they trusted her and let themselves be led inside to a table covered with a snow white cloth. The woman set out pancakes, with sugar to sprinkle on them, and milk to drink, and apples and nuts for dessert. After the meal she led them to a small room in which there were two soft beds, with clean white sheets and fluffy feather comforters. Hansel and Gretel lay down gratefully, and soon were fast asleep.

But the old woman was not what she seemed. She was not a kind lady who helped children in distress; she was a wicked witch instead, who had built her house out of lovely cakes, candies, and bread in order to lure children there so she could eat them.

The next morning, Hansel woke up to see the witch standing over him, rubbing her hands together and peering at him with her weak eyes. "A little thin," she cackled, poking him, "but we'll soon fatten you up. Girl!" she shouted at Gretel, while she pulled Hansel from his warm bed, "light the fire in my stove."

With that she took Hansel out to a small stable behind her house.

The stable was built of ordinary wood and thatch, not of food, and had a stall in it with bars like those of a cage. She locked Hansel in this stall, putting the key on a chain she wore around her waist.

"Fetch some water," she said to Gretel, as soon as she was inside again. "We will boil potatoes for your brother, to make him fat. We will make dumplings for him, and bread and cakes, and when he is fat, I will eat him."

Gretel began to cry, but the witch paid no attention, and made her work harder than any servant. Gretel had to cook fine food for the witch and for Hansel, but she herself got only crusts.

Every morning the witch went out to Hansel's stall and, blinking and peering, said, "Hansel, hold out your finger so I may see how fat you are getting." On the first day, Hansel did what he was told, but after that, realizing that the witch could see very little, he held out a thin stick instead. Each morning the witch felt the stick, shook her head, and said, "Surely he will grow fat soon. Gretel—more bread!"

But after a month had passed and Hansel was still no fatter, the witch grew impatient. "Gretel," she said one morning, "fill my big kettle with water, for today I will cook Hansel, no matter how thin he is."

Tears flowing down her cheeks, Gretel fetched the water, stopping at the stable to warn Hansel. "Maybe you can escape when she opens the door," Gretel whispered. "Maybe she won't be able to see well enough to grab you, and then you can run away."

"But what of you, little sister?" said Hansel. "I cannot run away and leave you here!"

"I will run, too," said Gretel, and so that was their plan.

But the witch had a plan of her own. "We will bake before we boil," she said, when Gretel came in with the water. "The fire is good and hot—just creep into the oven, Gretel, and see if it is hot enough, and if it is, we will put in the bread." And, indeed, there were three pans of bread dough on the table waiting to be baked. The witch, however, had no intention of

baking them—no, indeed; her plan was to shut the oven door on Gretel and bake her instead.

But Gretel was smarter than the witch; she knew the witch had never asked her to get inside the oven before to see if it was hot. "I don't understand," she said, pretending. "How am I to get into the oven?"

"Why, just climb in, silly girl," said the witch.

"Yes, but *how?*" Gretel persisted. "Head first, feet first, sideways—how? The opening looks so small!"

"Silly goose," said the witch, exasperated. "It is quite big enough—look, it is even big enough for me. You can get in this way." And the witch put her head and shoulders into the oven, demonstrating.

Gretel jumped forward and gave the witch a tremendous push with all her strength, sending her the rest of the way into the oven. Quickly, she seized the key from the witch's chain, slammed the heavy oven door tight shut, and ran out to the stable to unlock her brother's prison. "Hansel, Hansel, we're free!" she shouted, and told him she had put the witch into the oven.

Hansel leapt from the stall, and the two children embraced each other and danced around the stable. Then they went to the house and tore off great hunks of bread and cake to take with them when they left. They went inside and opened a large chest the witch kept in her room, and it was full of jewels and pearls. Hansel put as many in his pockets as he could, and Gretel tied some up in her apron, and they put more in two sacks that they found, and put the bread and cakes on top. "Now we must go," said Hansel. "Let us get as far as we can from the witch's house."

Again the children walked and walked for hours, and at last they came to the lake that they knew was not far from their cottage. "We must have walked all the way around it somehow," said Hansel. "It will take us days to walk around it again—and we might get lost once more. We will have to build a boat."

"No," said Gretel. "Look, there is another way across."

On the lake was swimming a large duck, who came when Gretel called her. Hansel climbed on her back, balancing his sack of jewels and food, and motioned to Gretel to sit beside him. "No," said Gretel, "she is not big enough to carry two. I will wait while you cross."

The duck took Hansel across the lake and came back for Gretel, and quacked at them softly as if saying good-bye when they left.

Now as they walked they began to recognize their surroundings. "Look," said Hansel, "there is the holly tree that has such pretty red berries in winter"—and, "Look," said Gretel, "there is the old hemlock we used to climb"—and before long they had come to their father's cottage. When they saw it, and their father outside, they ran and threw themselves into their father's arms. He hugged them close and laughed with joy, and told them how sad he had been while they were gone, and told them also that their selfish stepmother had died. Then when they went inside, Gretel emptied her sack and her apron, and Hansel his sack and his pockets, and there was plenty of food to put in the cupboard and there were jewels in every corner, enough to buy food for years and years and years, so that the woodcutter and his children need never be hungry again.

And they never were, nor did they ever have to trouble their minds anymore about being poor.

THE FISHERMAN AND HIS WIFE

Now once long ago near the shore of the sea there lived a fisherman and his wife—but they lived in a pigsty, and the wife was discontented. One day when the man was fishing, he suddenly felt a great tug upon his line, and after he pulled and pulled and pulled he brought up from the depths an enormous flounder, which is a flat fish with both its eyes on the same side.

"Fisherman," said the flounder, "cut me loose and throw me back, for I am not what I seem."

"What are you, then?" asked the fisherman, his knife in his hand.

"I am an enchanted prince," said the flounder, "and I would therefore not be good to eat. He who would buy me at the market would be angry with you for selling such tough, old meat."

"Well," said the fisherman, "I know nothing of that, but I do know that I have never seen a talking fish before, and therefore I will cut you loose and throw you back."

And he did.

"Husband," said the fisherman's wife when he returned home empty-handed at the end of the day, "have you caught nothing?"

"I have brought nothing home," the man said. "As to catching—I did catch a huge flounder." And he told her about the fish and what he had said.

"An enchanted prince!" cried the wife. "Did you not wish for anything?"

"Why, no," said the fisherman, surprised. "Why should I?"

"Well," said the wife, "one that has been enchanted and is in another shape has the power to grant wishes—and look at where we live, husband. Would you not prefer a nice little house to this filthy pigsty?"

The husband looked around at the mud and the straw and, although he knew his wife always wished for more than she had, he had to agree that a little house would be more comfortable. "Very well," he said to his wife, "I will go tomorrow and ask for a little house."

"No, go now," his wife said, "for you cannot be sure where the fish will be tomorrow."

So out the husband went, and the sea was less smooth than before, and showed shades of green and yellow amid its usual blue.

The fisherman, who had put his rod away, stood on the beach and cried:

> Flounder, swimming round and round,
> Cast yourself upon the ground.
> My wife, she wants a boon of thee:
> She would ever greater be.

Immediately the flounder rose to the surface and cast himself upon the beach, saying, "Well, fisherman, I thought you would be back. What does your wife wish?"

"She wishes," said the fisherman, "though I apologize for troubling you, for a little house instead of the pigsty in which we now live."

"Return to her," said the flounder, "and see what you will see."

So the fisherman walked back up the beach to where he lived, and found the sty no longer there, but in its place a little house, neat and clean and pretty. His wife was sitting in the front yard on a comfortable bench, lifting her face up to the sun.

"Well, now, wife," said the fisherman, "you have your wish, I see."

"Yes, indeed," she answered, smiling, and stood up. "Come inside," she said, "and admire our house." She led him in, first through a small porch, and then into a comfortable parlor with chairs and cushions and a cheerful fire burning on the hearth, and then into a bedroom with the finest of soft featherbeds and the stoutest of chests for their few clothes. And then she took him to the pantry, whose shelves were lined with jams and jellies and preserved fruit, and in whose cupboards were plenty of flour and sugar and salt, and then into the kitchen, where copper pots gleamed on hooks, and the best of tin utensils hung handily by the large iron stove. "This is splendid, wife," the fisherman said, well pleased, "splendid!"

"Ah, but wait," she said, leading him out the kitchen door into the back garden, in which grew flowers of every color and vegetables of every description and fruits and berries of all kinds. And in a small yard nearby scratched hens, and on a tiny pond, ducks swam.

"Well," said the husband, "we want for nothing, I see—except, of course, ocean fish, and those," he said, well content—for he enjoyed his work—"those I see I still must catch. But of all else," he told his wife as they went back inside, "we have enough and more."

"We will see," said the wife, frowning slightly as she cut bread for their supper.

For the next two weeks, all was well, except the wife frowned more as time progressed, and began sighing as she went about her housework, finding this or that wrong or difficult. "The fire in the stove singes my hair," she complained one day. "My poor back aches from carrying pails of water from the pond to wash our clothes," she said the next day, and that night she said, "It is such a bother to gather eggs every day from the hens"—and so on, until at the end of the two weeks she slammed their food upon the table and said, "There! Now I have done with cooking and cleaning in these cramped quarters and all by myself. You must go back to the flounder and ask him for a stone castle and for servants to care for it—for what will we do here when winter comes and the pond freezes and the garden is under the snow?"

"Wife," said the fisherman, "we managed quite well in our pigsty, and others manage well in houses less fine than this one. You will put up food from the garden for the winter, and if caring for the house is too much

for you, why, I will help you myself, or we will
to come."

"No," said the wife, "for it is not that alone. I
here. There is not enough space; I cannot breathe!"

The fisherman tried to argue against that, but h.
listen, so at last he agreed reluctantly to go back to the flo

He walked slowly, though, shaking his head, for he 1
flounder would think him and his wife ungrateful. The ocean
dark blue-green with purple streaks—but its surface still moved
the waves rolled steadily in without breaking.

The fisherman stood by the water's edge and cried:

> Flounder, swimming round and round,
> Cast yourself upon the ground.
> My wife, she wants a boon of thee:
> She would even greater be.

The flounder rose as before and came out upon the sand, saying, "Well, and what does she want now?"

"Oh, flounder," the fisherman said with many apologies, "alas, she says her house is too small and that she needs servants; she would like, please, a stone castle and people to tend it for her."

"Return to her," said the flounder, "and see what you will see."

So the fisherman turned back to the little house, but found instead a great stone castle, with all as his wife had envisioned. She met him outside, standing upon the drawbridge that spanned the moat, and servants opened the doors for them as they went in. The great hall had a gleaming marble floor, and woven tapestries of red and blue and green were upon the walls. Warm fires crackled merrily at both ends of the hall; golden chairs stood about, and polished tables, and crystal chandeliers sparkled from the ceilings. On the floors were thick carpets of deep red and royal blue and [illegible] the fisherman and his wife wanted to eat, liveried servants brought them sweet wine and so many wonderful dishes they could only nibble at each one if they wished to taste them all. Outside in the courtyard was a stable full of fine horses, and next to it a carriage house, and behind it a barn for milk cows. Nearby was a garden in which were exotic flowers and fruit trees and vegetables from every corner of the earth, and adjoining that was a beautiful park, half a mile long on each side, with paths and tree-bordered avenues and ponds and pavilions and gazebos. In the park roamed deer and stags and hares, and from its trees sang bright-feathered birds.

The fisherman gasped to see such splendor, and could not believe it was for him and his wife to enjoy all by themselves. But she assured him that it was, and that the suits of soft, warm cloth in the bedroom chests were his alone, and that he need fish no more but could sit every day in whatever place he chose—castle, park, or garden, or he could ride in one of his carriages or upon one of his horses, or go hunting in his park. "No, wife," the fisherman said, "I would miss my old comfortable clothes and my work; I will dress as I am accustomed to dress, and go every day to fish as I always have."

"Perhaps that is wise," the wife said, a small frown furrowing her forehead.

"What now?" asked the fisherman. "Surely we can be content with all this splendor for the rest of our lives."

"Perhaps," said the wife. "We will see."

The next morning the wife awoke as the sun rose, and went to the window and looked out over the land. The castle was so high that from it she could see far and wide, and she looked out over hills and gently rolling green fields on the side opposite the sea. She sighed then and, turning from the window, shook her husband awake and bade him look out also.

"Yes," he said, "a lovely view. Now I must hurry; the sun is climbing higher and as you know, the fish bite best before it is full up."

"Ah, husband," the wife said, gazing out over the fields and the hills, "would it not be a fine thing to be king over all that we can see from our castle? For what good is a castle if it does not stand ready to defend its own kingdom?"

"Hush, wife," said the fisherman, pulling on his old boots, "do not speak so! I have no wish to be king."

"Well, if you do not," said the wife stubbornly, "I do. Go back to the flounder, and ask him to make me king."

"Wife, wife," said the fisherman, reaching for his rod, "I cannot do that."

"But why not?" she asked. "He has given us all else we have asked for. Why not one more thing? Go," she commanded, as if she were king already. "Go at once; I would be king!"

So the fisherman, seeing that she would have her way no matter what he said, sighed and, after finding his way through the many rooms and halls and alcoves of the castle, crossed the drawbridge and walked again upon the shore.

This time the sea was gray, and the waves rolled and pounded dangerously, and the water smelled vile. The man shivered as he stood and cried:

Flounder, swimming round and round,
Cast yourself upon the ground.
My wife, she wants a boon of thee:
She would even greater be.

The flounder appeared as before, and went out upon the sand, and said, "Well, fisherman, and what does she want now?"

"Oh, flounder," said the man sadly, "forgive me. Her wish is foolish and impossible—alas, she wishes to be king."

"Return to her," said the flounder, "and see what you will see."

So the fisherman returned, and found the castle grown into a magnificent palace, with everything larger and more splendid than before. The palace was topped with a magnificent tower, and the moat was walled with battlements and had become wider, with a heavy drawbridge that was lifted by great, straining iron chains trimmed with gold. Sentinels stood on guard all around, and a military band trumpeted and drummed as the fisherman approached. Inside, the walls as well as the floor were now of marble. The hangings were cloth-of-gold, and the chairs were covered in purple velvet with gold tassles, and diamonds hung glittering from the chandeliers. The fisherman found his wife seated on a throne encrusted with rubies, sapphires, and emeralds, and on her head was a golden crown, and in her hand was a jeweled scepter. Rings sparkled from each of her fingers and seven precious necklaces decorated her throat. Ladies-in-waiting stood by the throne ready to serve her, each one shorter than the other so that they looked like steps descending from either side of their mistress.

"Wife," said the fisherman, bowing, "so now you are king."

"Yes," she said. "Now I am king."

The fisherman did not know what to say, so he stood in front of the throne for a long time, gazing at his wife and at the magnificence of her court. In a while he said, "And now you have all that can be had; you are the richest and most powerful in the land, so we will now live in this fashion, content, for the rest of our days. I will go every day to fish, and you will sit here and rule."

"You may do as you wish," said his wife haughtily, "but as for me. . . ." She sighed. "Just sitting on this throne is not enough," she told him. "The time goes slowly—there is not enough to do. If I ruled more, there would be more for me to attend to. You must go back to the flounder. Oh, if only I had the power to command great legions and send messengers all over the world—not just within my own small kingdom!"

"But wife," the fisherman began—but she interrupted.

"Go, husband," she commanded, holding out a hand heavy with rings. "Go back to the flounder and tell him I would be emperor."

"Emperor!" cried the fisherman. "But that is not possible! There is an emperor already, and there cannot be two. The flounder cannot grant that wish!"

"Silence!" said the wife. "I am king, and therefore I may command what I wish. If the flounder can make me king, he can also make me emperor. And I will have him do so; I command it. Go—go this minute."

So the fisherman went, but on the way he muttered to himself. "Alas, alas, where will this end? Surely the flounder cannot make her emperor! It is shameless of her; it will end badly. And the poor flounder will wear himself out granting all these wishes."

The wind blew as the fisherman stood by the water's edge, and the sea turned black and boiled upon the shore, sending huge waves to break at the fisherman's feet. He had never seen the sea so angry, and he trembled as he watched it. Then, with the water swirling about his feet, he cried:

Flounder, swimming round and round,
Cast yourself upon the ground.
My wife, she wants a boon of thee:
She would even greater be.

The flounder came out of the boiling sea onto the land and said crossly, "Well, well, and what does she want *now?*"

The fisherman did not like to say, but he knew he must, so he looked away from the fish and said humbly, "Oh, flounder, she wishes an absurdity—she wishes to be emperor!"

"Return to her," said the flounder, "and see what you will see."

The fisherman went slowly home, and now the outside of the palace was marble as well as the inside, and soldiers from many lands marched about. The inside of the palace was hung with gold and diamonds, and for servants there were dukes and barons and counts and other noble folk. Soft music wafted from every corner as if magically borne on the air, and whole

oxen roasted on the kitchen hearths. There was a great coming and going of messengers, and the doors, which were flung open as the fisherman walked through the rooms, were made of gold, and in front of each one knelt a young page, endlessly polishing.

At last the fisherman found his wife, seated on a throne cut from a single piece of gold, and so high he had to tip back his head to see her. When he did, his eyes were near-blinded by the splendor of her jewels. In one hand she held the scepter, and in the other, the imperial orb, signifying that she ruled over all the world. In two rows beside her stood guardsmen. The ones closest to her were giants—but still no higher than her throne—and the ones farthest away were dwarfs, so again they were arranged like steps.

Princes and dukes crowded around the throne, asking for favors. The fisherman waited his turn among them and at last was able to speak. "Wife," he said, "I see that you have enough to do now that you are emperor. So now you will be content, I am sure. And as you will have no further need of me, I will leave the palace and spend the rest of my days fishing."

"Husband," she said, "you cannot spend your days fishing; you must return to the flounder, for as emperor I rule only over worldly things. I would rule over *everything,* and so I must be pope."

The fisherman turned pale and the sweat stood out on his brow. "What is it you are saying, wife? You know full well there can be only one pope in all of Christendom; the flounder has not the power to make you pope!"

"You make me tired," said the wife. "Go immediately to the flounder, for I would be pope this very moment."

"No, wife," said the fisherman, "no, I will not. It is too much; you must be content with being emperor."

But the wife raised her hand toward the guardsmen and they stepped forward, from the largest giant to the tiniest dwarf, and the fisherman was afraid and therefore went, though his knees were like water and his whole body trembled.

The wind blew fiercely over the land and drove the thundering sea upon the shore, and the clouds fled before the wind. The leaves were torn from the trees and toward evening the water rose in great towers and crashed onto the land. The fisherman saw ships tossed about like toys, and great stones rolling about in the sea. The sky was black, but not quite black throughout; there was one small, bright patch of blue overhead, edged with white clouds touched with gold.

> Flounder, swimming round and round,
> Cast yourself upon the ground.
> My wife, she wants a boon of thee:
> She would even greater be.

"What now?" asked the flounder, his tail lashing as if in anger.

"She would be pope," said the fisherman, turning red, "but I know you cannot. . . ."

"Return to her," said the flounder, "and see what you will see."

And when the fisherman returned, there was what looked like a large church where the palace had been, and all around it were what appeared to be small palaces. The guards were dressed in gold and crimson, and inside cardinals and bishops and priests went about their business soberly. The walls of what had formerly been the great hall were hung with beautiful paintings, and noble statues stood in deep-cut niches. The panes of the windows held stained-glass pictures of great beauty, and from above, choirs sang. The fisherman found his wife on an even higher throne, clothed in magnificent white robes trimmed with gold, and on her head was a golden miter, studded with jewels; all else was even more splendid than before. On each side of the fisherman's wife were rows of descending candles, the tallest nearly as high as her throne, and the smallest, a tiny kitchen candle. An emperor and a king knelt before her, among the dukes and princes, kissing her shoe.

"Wife," said the fisherman, "you are now pope, are you not?"

"Yes," she answered. "Yes, I am now pope."

"And since you are pope," he said, "you can be no higher. Well, at last it is over, and I may fish in peace."

But his wife sat stiffly, and did not speak.

"Wife," he said again, "be content; you can go no higher."

"We will see," said his wife. But she was silent for the rest of the day and evening, so the fisherman was full of hope when he went to bed.

He himself slept well, exhausted, but his wife tossed restlessly all the night long, for she wished to be greater still but could not think how. Many hours passed before the moon set, and many more before the sun rose. When it did, the wife saw the sky brighten and then glow with reds and yellows, and she remembered how the moon the night before had touched all with silver. She said to herself, "Why could I not order the sun and the moon to rise and set and thus have day or night whenever I wished?" So she went to her husband and shook him awake, saying, "Husband, husband, wake up; you must return to the flounder!"

Horrified, the fisherman sat up in bed, rubbing the sleep from his eyes. "How so?" he said. "For there is nothing higher on this earth than pope and you are that already; be content!"

"No," said the wife, pointing to the reddening sky, "I wish to be as God is; I wish to command the sun and the moon—nay, and the stars, too."

The husband shook his head, thinking sleep must be muddying his mind. Then he laughed heartily and said, "Do you know what nonsense I thought you just spoke?" he said. "I thought you said you wished to be even as God is!"

"I did," said the wife. "That is exactly what I said, and exactly what I want. You must return to the flounder this instant. If I cannot command the sun and the moon to rise—if I must see them rising and not have commanded them myself—I will not be able to bear it, and I shall be miserable for the rest of my days." She began then to weep, and when the fisherman remained as motionless as a stone, she dried her tears and cast on him a look so terrible that he shuddered. "Go at once," she said, seeing him weaken, "go this instant and tell the flounder that I would be as God is."

"Alas," said the fisherman, rising out of bed and then falling to his knees in despair, "alas, I beseech you, wife, go on as you have been; be pope and be content with that."

But the wife became angry, and in her rage she kicked her husband and tore her hair and screamed until he thought she would go mad.

So at last he gave in and ran outside, where a great storm was putting all the world into turmoil. He could scarcely walk in the wind, and all around him trees fell over and houses were torn from their foundations. The very mountains trembled and rocks rolled down their sides into the sea. The thunder crashed and great, jagged tongues of lightning licked the sea. The waves were as tall as mountains themselves and shook the land as they broke upon it, spewing foam for many miles. The fisherman could not hear his own words when he cried:

Flounder, swimming round and round,
Cast yourself upon the ground.
My wife, she wants a boon of thee:
She would even greater be.

The flounder tossed himself onto the beach on the crest of a huge wave and fixed the fisherman with his eyes and said, "Well, and what now?" and the fisherman, his knees collapsing beneath him, whispered, "Alas, alas, flounder; she wants to be like God!"

"Return to her," said the flounder, turning and leaping back into the waves. "Return to her and—see—what—you—will see!"

So the fisherman crept home, and found his wife back again in the pigsty, and there, if old age has not yet claimed them, they are living still.

THE VALIANT LITTLE TAILOR

ONCE on a lovely summer's morning a little tailor sat in his shop making a jacket trimmed with fancy braid. It was such a handsome garment that the tailor was most glad to work upon it, and he sang merrily as he sewed.

Outside in the street a peasant woman passed by, balancing a huge basket on her sturdy shoulders. "Jams, fine jams!" she called, as she walked slowly along. "Elderberry, blackberry, and current! Strawberry, raspberry, and peach! Cherry! Apricot! Minted crabapple!"

"Mmmmm," said the tailor to himself, "just the thing to go with the new loaf I bought on my way to the shop. My good woman!" he called, going to the door. "Dear woman, come here, for I shall buy your jam!"

The woman, hoping that he meant he was going to buy all of her jam at once, or nearly all, ran as lightly as she could up the steps to the tailor's shop, and set down her basket. "Now, sir, what will you have?" she asked, beaming. "One of each perhaps? Or half a dozen of your favorite, and a few extras for the wife and children?"

"Well, now," said the tailor, "well, now, let us see." Carefully, he picked up each jar and held it to the light. "Ho—hmmm," he said, examining each one carefully. "Aha—yes, indeed"—until the woman grew impatient, and shifted her weight first to one foot, then to the other.

"This one seems good," the tailor said, peering closely at the way the sunlight made the colors glow and shimmer in a jar of blackberry jam.

"Quite good indeed, sir," said the woman. "Fine, in fact. And as it happens, I have a good supply of blackberry—oh, an excellent supply, for it was a good year. Why, I have even more jars at home that I would be delighted to fetch for you. . . ."

"Oh, no, no, no, my dear woman," said the little tailor, "no need, no need. Why, even one jar will be too much for me, for I have no wife and no little ones either. No, no, no, just be so good as to weigh me out four ounces of this beautiful jam—here, we can put it in this little dish—and if it be as much as a quarter of a pound, why, I will take that gladly."

The woman looked surprised and then angry, and she grumbled about opening the jar and then having to close it up again—for who would want to buy a half-filled jar except another customer like this one? But in the end she agreed, and went on her way, shaking her head and muttering, while the little tailor rubbed his hands together in eager anticipation of the feast he was about to have.

He took the fresh, crusty-brown loaf from his cupboard and cut himself a thick slice, and spread the jam liberally over it. "Mmmmm," he said, his mouth watering, "how good that looks! But first I will finish this jacket—for a good pleasure is often improved by waiting."

The little tailor put the bread and jam down beside him and again picked up the jacket, humming as he stitched.

Now the jam was indeed good jam, and very sweet, and soon its fragrance drew all the flies in the shop, who swarmed above the slice of bread and then settled on it in great numbers.

"Hey, now!" shouted the little tailor, seeing the flies when he put aside the jacket and reached for his bread. "Whose bread and jam is this, I might ask? Away, rude beasts, begone!" He waved his hand above the bread; several flies flew off, but the rest remained.

"Well, I will soon give you what for," the little tailor said, and he seized a stiff scrap of brocade from his fabric corner, and swatted the flies with it. And when he lifted up the cloth, seven flies lay flattened under it.

"Seven!" the little tailor said, admiring his own work. "Seven at once, imagine that! Everyone must hear of this!" And so he made himself a belt, and on it he embroidered in large letters:

SEVEN DOWNED AT ONCE!

That very afternoon the little tailor fastened his new belt around his waist, closed up his shop, and set forth into the world. "For," he told the owner of the jacket, delivering it on his way, "a man who can down seven at once should not keep himself in a shop, cutting and stitching."

On his way also, the little tailor stopped in at his own house to see what would be useful to take with him. "This cheese is just the thing," he said, finding a piece in his larder, and putting it in his pocket. There seemed nothing else useful except a bird which had caught itself in a bush outside the front door; he put the bird in his pocket along with the cheese. And whistling cheerily, the little tailor set off down the road.

In a while the road sloped upward, crossing a mountain, but the tailor was as wiry as he was small, and he climbed it easily. At the very top sat an enormous giant, looking out over the world. Most other folks would have fled in terror, or crept soundlessly away, but tne little tailor was as bold as he was wiry, so he went right up to the giant and said, "How do you do, friend! I see you are looking out over the very world I am journeying into; would you like to come along?"

The giant looked down from his great height at the little tailor and, sneering, said, "What? Go with you, you miserable insect? Why, you are so small you are nothing at all! If I sneezed I would blow you into the next kingdom and beyond!"

"Is that so?" said the little tailor, and he opened his coat and showed the giant his belt.

" 'Seven—downed—at—once!' " the giant spelled out slowly, and then he blinked in surprise, for he thought the words meant seven *men*. "Well," he said begrudgingly, "perhaps you are not quite so weak as you look. But we will try your strength first." So saying, the giant stooped and picked up a heavy stone from the mountaintop, and squeezed it until drops of water fell from it. "You do the same," said the giant. "If you are as strong as you say, it will be easy."

"It will, indeed," said the little tailor, and he stooped, pretending to pick up a stone but, in truth, fetching the cheese from his pocket. "See," he said to the giant, holding the cheese so that most of it was hidden under his fingers. "See how easily I do the same"—and he squeezed the cheese until water fairly ran from it upon the ground.

"Humph," said the giant. "Humph." Then he picked up another stone and, drawing back his mighty arm, hurled it out over the forests and green fields and villages below. "Now, little man, let me see you do the same."

"Well done," said the little tailor as if in admiration, "very well done. But of course we both *did* see your stone come down to the ground again, though it did indeed travel far. Now I will throw one that will go so far it will not come down at all." And the little tailor stooped again as if picking up another stone, but this time bringing out the bird. Drawing back his arm as the giant had done, he let loose the bird, and the bird, overjoyed to be out of the tailor's dark and stuffy pocket, soared into the air. The giant and the little tailor watched till they could see it no longer, and then the tailor said, "How do you like that?"

"Not bad," said the giant. "It is true that you can throw, and that you can squeeze, but let us see if you can also carry." He led the little tailor partway down the other side of the mountain and into a forest, where there was a huge oak tree lying upon the ground. "If you are so strong," the giant said, "you will be able to help me carry this tree to where I live, so I may use it for firewood."

"Certainly," said the little tailor, "what an easy job! You take the trunk, and go first," he went on. "I will take the heavy part—the branches and leaves."

The giant lifted the trunk upon his shoulder and the tailor climbed up among the thick leaves and sat upon a branch. "Ready!" he called, and the giant, grunting, moved forward. Once he tried to look around at the tailor, but there were so many branches in the way he could see nothing but them. "How do you fare, tailor?" he called out, gasping with the weight of the tree, and the tailor, in a fresh, clear voice answered, "Oh, very well, friend, very well; in fact, can you not walk a little faster? My feet are falling asleep with inactivity."

The giant tried to walk faster, grunting harder, but the tailor for his part began whistling, as if there were nothing to the job at all.

At last the giant, with a mighty groan, called, "Tailor, I can go no further. My arms are shaking, and I must drop my end."

Just in time, the tailor hopped down from his branch and put both his arms around the top of the trunk as if he had been carrying it all along. "My, my," he said, as the giant sank upon the ground to rest, "and you *look* so strong—yet you cannot even carry a little tree!"

When the giant had rested, they continued on their way, and when they came to a cherry tree heavy with fruit, the giant smacked his lips and said, "If you are as hungry as I after our labors, you are near starvation. Here—I will hold the tree down while you gather some fruit, and then you may do the same for me." The giant pulled the tree down and bade the tailor take hold of a branch and keep it steady; the tailor did, but then the giant let go, and the tree sprang upright, tossing the tailor high into the air.

When the tailor came down again, he jumped up and brushed himself off to show he was unhurt, but even so the giant beamed triumphantly and said, "What? What? You are so strong, yet you cannot hold down a little cherry tree?"

"Is that what you think?" said the tailor. "Holding down a cherry tree is nothing to a man who has downed seven at once. No, my friend, I jumped over the tree because there are hunters approaching, and one shot came straight at us—did you not hear it? But I suppose you could not jump as high as I did—a pity, for here comes another shot!"

The giant tried to jump over the tree, but he could only get partway up, and his coat caught on a branch. There he dangled until the tailor pretended to shake him down—but, in truth, he waited until the giant's coat was about to tear from bearing such great weight, and then the tailor leaned against the tree as if shaking it.

"Well," said the giant, when he was back upon the ground and had put himself to rights, "if you are as brave as you are strong, you will not mind spending the night with my family; come with me to my cave."

The tailor agreed, and on they walked till they came to a huge cave that was taller than the tallest castle—and even so, the giant had to stoop to enter.

Inside, there were other giants, sitting by the fire and eating. The youngest and smallest held a whole roasted sheep in one hand.

When they had all eaten, the giant showed the tailor where he was to sleep—it was a huge bed, as big as an entire ship. It was so big that the little tailor felt lost in it, so he curled up cozily in one corner. At midnight, the giant got up out of his own bed, saying, "Now I will finish him—for I cannot allow a creature smaller than myself to be so strong." He took a heavy iron bar in his hand and smote the bed a mighty blow, splitting it in two. But the tailor was safe in his corner.

At dawn the giants went into the forest to look for food, thinking the little tailor was done for. But as the sun came full up, he strolled up to them, smiling and saying, "Ah, what a fine sleep I had—what a very comfortable bed—except for. . . ."

The giants were so terrified, and so afraid that the tailor would now do to them what he had done to the seven, that they fled before he had finished speaking.

Chuckling heartily, the little tailor went on, for he was enjoying his adventures despite their danger. In a while he came to a royal palace with a grassy courtyard, so, since he was by now quite tired, he stretched out comfortably under a tree and fell asleep. While he lay there, some of the king's servants spied him and inspected him curiously, as they did all strangers.

" 'Seven downed at once!' " said one, reading the words on the little tailor's belt. "My, my! I wonder what such a great warrior is doing here—for we are not even at war right now."

"Still, he must be a great warrior indeed," said another servant, "to down seven at once. We should take him to the king—for think how useful he would be if there *were* a war!"

The servants ran to the king, who sent his most trusted courtier out to wait till the mighty stranger woke up and then to offer him a place of honor in his army. The courtier stood quietly beside the little tailor till he stretched, yawned, and opened his eyes. Then with great respect the courtier said, "Mighty warrior, I am come from the king to offer you a place in his royal army."

"Splendid," said the little tailor. "That is the very reason why I came here. Lead me to the king, my good man."

The king received the little tailor as if he were a hero, and made him general of half his army, and gave him a beautiful house to live in.

But the soldiers who were to serve under him were not pleased. "How can we follow such a man?" they said to each other. "If we displease him, he will kill us all, seven at a time, till there are none of us left." So they went to the king and begged him to reconsider. "We cannot do it, sire," the soldiers said. "We cannot fight under a commander whom we fear more than we fear any enemy. If you do not ask him to leave, we will be forced to leave ourselves."

Now the king had a terrible dilemma, for he did not wish to lose half his royal army—and yet he, too, feared the little tailor now and was afraid that if he dismissed him, the tailor would strike him dead along with six of his court, and then down the rest by sevens till none were left.

At last he felt he had thought of a safe plan to rid himself of the little tailor, and so he sent his same trusted courtier to speak to him. "Good sir," said the courtier, "there is, as you know, no war at present, but the king does have need of your services nonetheless. In the forest near here there dwell two giants who do nothing but murder and plunder the peasants of this kingdom. Many brave men have tried to conquer these giants but all have failed. But the king believes that a man who can down seven at once can surely down two, and begs you to rid us of these monsters. When they lie dead, the king will give you his only daughter in marriage, and half his kingdom as well. And his majesty, in his generosity, has decreed that you may take one hundred horsemen with you to assist you."

"Well, well," said the little tailor, "what a fine offer! It is not every day one is offered a princess and half a kingdom! I will willingly slay your giants—and never fear," he said to the hundred horsemen who trembled behind the courtier. "I will not need your help. He who has downed seven at once, as the king so wisely says, need have no fear of two."

So the little tailor went off by himself into the forest, where he found both giants sleeping under a tree, snoring mightily. The little tailor filled his pockets with stones and climbed the tree, settling on a branch just above the sleepers. "And now for some fun," he said, dropping a stone on the elbow of one of the giants, who stirred but did not wake. "Ho, ho," chuckled the little tailor. "And now again," and he let drop another stone, this one onto the giant's chest. And so he continued, stone after stone, till at last the giant awoke and shook his fellow giant awake, also. "What do you think you're doing?" he bellowed. "Why are you hitting me?"

"I am not hitting you," said the other giant angrily. "As you saw, I was asleep till you woke me."

"No one else is here," said the first giant. "Therefore it must have been you, hitting me in your sleep."

"I tell you I was not!" shouted the second giant—and they argued thus for a time but at last, since both were sleepy, they gave it up and closed their eyes again, turning their backs on each other.

The little tailor waited till they were both snoring again, and then he dropped his biggest stone, hard, on the first giant's chest. Instantly the giant woke up and seized his comrade. "I told you not to hit me!" he roared, and he shook the second giant back and forth until the ground trembled.

"And I told you I did not hit you!" cried the second giant, twisting away from the first and then wrestling him to the ground.

Mayer

On and on they fought, pulling up whole trees in their rage and stamping great craters in the forest floor. And at last they both fell down dead at the same moment.

"What good luck," the tailor said, leaping down from his hiding place, "that they did not pull up *my* tree, or I should have had to jump like a squirrel to another—but I am wiry and quick, and could easily have done it."

Then, to make things look right, the tailor gave each giant a stab or two in the chest with his sword and sauntered out of the forest and back to the palace. "It was hard," he said to the king, "but I have done it; the giants fought me so hard we tore up half the forest, but they will give you no more trouble."

"Go and see," said the king, and the horsemen rode trembling into the forest and came back and reported to the king that all was as the tailor had said.

"And now," said the tailor, "as I have fulfilled your request and not even lost one hair of my head in doing it, it is time for you to give me my reward."

"Ah, as to that," said the king uncomfortably—for he had no wish to give up his daughter or half his kingdom—"while you were battling the giants, a unicorn which has plagued us in years past returned and tore up several farms. We cannot have a royal wedding till we are rid of it; you must catch it first and then we will speak of rewards."

"Pah!" said the little tailor, "what is one unicorn? Two giants were little enough; this is even less for one who has downed seven at once."

The little tailor asked for a rope and an axe and with these as his sole companions he went in the direction the king pointed out to him. Soon he heard a great hammering of hooves and the unicorn rushed into the clearing where the tailor was, lowering its gleaming horn at him. The little tailor crouched at the edge of the clearing, near a tree, saying to himself, "Patience, patience, wait for the moment," and he did not move even as the unicorn ran toward him. But when the unicorn was almost upon him, the little tailor leapt behind the tree, and the unicorn thundered against it, and its horn stuck fast in the trunk. "Now I have you!" cried the little tailor, and put the rope about the unicorn's neck. With his axe he freed the horn from the tree and then he led the beast to the king.

"Ah, well," said the king, hedging again, "yes, that is wonderful—wonderful, what you have done. But, alas, while you were gone, a wild boar attacked my royal huntsmen and caused no end of damage; if you can rid us of him, then you may have my daughter and half my kingdom."

"That will be fun," said the tailor, hiding his annoyance. "A boar is a bit of a match for most folk, but not for me—not for one who has downed seven at once." And off he went into the forest, in the direction the remaining huntsmen told him to go.

Soon the boar appeared, foaming at the mouth and eyeing the little tailor malevolently and tossing its sharp tusks. For a moment it appeared that all was lost, for the boar charged the tailor before he had devised a careful plan. Luckily there was a chapel nearby and the tailor fled inside, leaving the door wide open, and in the nick of time leapt out a window. The boar, who had followed the tailor inside, was too heavy and clumsy to follow him out the window, and as it stood beneath the window gnashing its teeth, the tailor ran around to the front of the chapel again and slammed the door tight shut.

And so the boar was caught, and the tailor went again to the king. "Now, your majesty," he said with great firmness, "I have done three great deeds for you, all for the same reward, and methinks it is time for your part of the bargain."

"Yes, yes," said the king. "To be sure. However, just a few moments ago . . ."

Seeing that the king was about to set him another task, the little tailor opened his coat, showing the words on his belt, and then reached for his sword.

" . . . just a few moments ago," the king said hastily, trying not to shrink back in fear as plainly as his courtiers were doing, "just now, in fact, my daughter was saying to me that she wished the wedding to take place without delay."

The little tailor smiled and buttoned his coat. The king called for his daughter, and soon the wedding was performed with proper royal splendor. The little tailor then found himself a king's heir, with half a kingdom to command.

But one night soon after, the princess heard her husband murmuring in his sleep, and she bent closer to listen. "That is fine cloth," she heard him say, "fine for a doublet; yes, I will have it ready by Thursday next, and the pantaloons as well."

What? thought the princess angrily. What kind of talk is this for a warrior?

And she listened for several nights more, and always the tailor talked in his sleep in the same vein—about fabrics and pins and tape measures and beeswax and needles.

When there was no doubt in her mind at all about what her husband truly was, the princess went to her father the king in anger and demanded that he get rid of the tailor and find her a husband who would not be beneath her.

"There, there, my dear," the king said—for he was glad of the opportunity to rid himself at last of his dangerous son-in-law—"calm yourself. Go to bed as usual tonight, and I shall station some of my soldiers outside your door. When your husband has fallen asleep, let them in. I will have them tie him up firmly in his sleep and put him on a ship that will take him to the ends of the earth."

One young page boy, however, who was standing nearby, overheard the king's plan, and, as the little tailor had mended his doublet for him once before the king had noticed he had carelessly torn it, he ran directly to the tailor and told him what he had heard. "Never fear," said the tailor,

"I will take care of that, and of the problem itself for good and all."

That night the tailor went to bed as usual, and pretended not to notice the soldiers assembling noisily outside his door—for though they were not the soldiers the king had first put under the tailor's command, they had heard of him and were afraid. The tailor pretended to fall asleep and soon his wife went outside and signaled the soldiers to enter. But before they had gone two steps, the little tailor, pretending to stir in his sleep, said in a loud voice, "Yes, yes, fine cloth for a duke's robes, but no good for a soldier's garb. I know what is best for military wear—for did I not down seven at once? And did I not kill two giants and capture one unicorn and imprison one wild boar? After all that, who am I to fear those who are standing outside my door?"

That was all the trembling soldiers needed to hear; as one man they turned and fled.

And so the princess remained with the tailor after all, and later came to admire him; in time, they were happy together. The tailor one day became king and she, queen, and they reigned in peace for many a year—for no one dared disturb the realm of the man who had downed seven at once!

LITTLE BRIAR ROSE

A LONG time ago there lived a king and queen who had a beautiful palace with many rooms and countless servants, along with spotted hounds, noble horses, gentle doves, and great riches—but no children. Scarcely a day passed but what one or the other of them didn't say, "Oh, if only we had a child!" But the years went by, and they remained childless.

One warm summer day the queen went wading among the lily pads in a secluded pool. "Alas," she said sadly, "if only I had a child."

A frog, sitting nearby on his lily pad, heard the queen's lament, and swam up to her, saying, "Your majesty, your patience will be rewarded. Before another year has passed, you will have a daughter."

Within the year the frog's promise came true, and the queen had a beautiful baby girl, whom she and the king named Briar Rose. The king was so happy that he ordered a great feast, and for days the servants scrubbed and polished, baked and roasted, until all was in readiness. The king and queen prepared the guest list, inviting all their kinsmen and kinswomen, and all their friends, and all the noble lords and ladies of their acquaintance. "We should invite the Wise Women as well," said the king, "so that they will always be kind to little Briar Rose."

"You are right," said the queen, "but you know they will eat only from golden plates."

"Well," said the king, "what of it? We have twelve golden plates."

"Yes," said the queen, "but there are thirteen Wise Women in our kingdom."

The king frowned, and thought, and at last said, "We will invite only twelve of the Wise Women, then." And that is what they did.

At last the great day came. Delicious fragrances filled the air, and the palace shone and sparkled as brightly as did the rich clothes of the royal guests. Little Briar Rose smiled from her cradle and, after the feast was done, the Wise Women passed by her one by one to give her their gifts.

"I give the king's daughter virtue," said the first Wise Woman.

"And I give her lasting beauty," said the second.

"And I, riches," said the third, and the others added their gifts until Briar Rose had been promised everything that one could wish for.

But when the eleventh Wise Woman had given her gift to little Briar Rose, there was a loud noise outside the great hall, and the thirteenth Wise Woman stormed in. "How dare you hold a feast without me!" she cried, and went straight to the cradle as if to add her gift to those of the others. Instead she said cruelly, "I give the king's daughter death; in her fifteenth year she will prick herself with a spindle, and fall down dead." And, without saying a word more, she turned and left the room.

The queen gasped and picked Briar Rose up, holding her close; the king put his arms around her. The guests stood in stunned silence. Then the twelfth Wise Woman, who had not yet given her gift, came forward, and said sadly, "I cannot undo what my evil sister has done, but I can soften it. Briar Rose shall not fall down dead in her fifteenth year; she will only sleep, deeply, for a hundred years."

"A hundred years!" said the king. "But we will all be gone when she awakes."

"Very well," said the gentle Wise Woman. "If you wish it, you and all the others in your palace may also sleep for the same hundred years."

"I wish it," said the king, and the queen nodded. The servants, who dared not oppose the king, nodded also.

Even so, the next morning the king sent his messengers all over the kingdom to order that every spindle be burned, and that no more be made or brought into the kingdom ever again.

The years passed, and Briar Rose grew up to be as virtuous, and as beautiful, and as rich, as the Wise Women had promised. She was so lovely, modest, good-natured, and wise that everyone who saw her loved her.

On Briar Rose's fifteenth birthday, the king and queen were called away on urgent business, and Briar Rose was left alone in the palace except for the servants. After a while she tired of her needlework and her golden ball and her books, so she decided to explore those parts of the palace that she had never seen. There were many rooms which her parents kept closed except when a great hunt or feast made the palace overflow with guests.

For hours, Briar Rose roamed through the palace, opening doors and fingering dusty draperies. At last, when it seemed there was nothing left that she had not seen, she came to a small door at the end of a dark hallway and, opening it, she found a narrow, winding staircase. "Why, this must go up inside one of those towers I can see from outside," she said, and immediately started climbing the stairs.

At the very top was another small door—locked, but with a rusty key in it. Briar Rose turned the key and the door sprung open.

There, in a little cobwebby room containing a bed and a chest and a stool, sat an old woman with a spindle, busily spinning flax.

"Good day, old mother," said Briar Rose politely, "are you one of my father's servants? I don't believe I have seen you before." She looked curiously at the thread that flowed from the strange object the woman held—for, of course, Briar Rose had never seen a spindle. "What are you doing?" she asked the woman.

"I am spinning," said the old woman, nodding her head in time to the rhythm of her hands.

"And what is that object that rattles around so merrily?" asked Briar Rose.

"Why, child," said the old woman, "that is a spindle. Would you like to learn how to use it?"

"Oh, yes," said Briar Rose, and she took the spindle from the old woman so eagerly that she pricked her finger with it.

And in the very moment that she felt the prick, she fell down upon

Mayer

the bed that stood in the little room, and lay there in a deep sleep.

At the very same moment, everyone else in the palace fell into a deep sleep also, no matter what they were doing. The king and queen, who had just come home and entered the great hall, sank into sleep on the threshold, and the whole of their court with them. The horses went to sleep in the stable, as did the spotted hounds in the yard, the doves upon the roof, and the flies on the walls. Even the fire that was flaming on the hearth became quiet and slept. The roast left off sizzling, and the cook, who was just going to box the ears of the scullery boy, let him go and went to sleep. The kitchen maid fell asleep over a black hen she was plucking. And the wind died, and on the trees before the palace not a leaf moved.

As time passed, although every living thing inside the palace slept, the thorn hedge that surrounded the palace yard grew higher and thicker. When it had reached the height of the highest tower, it closed over the top of the palace, till nothing could be seen, not even the flag on the roof. But the story of the beautiful sleeping princess Briar Rose spread far and wide.

For many years, princes who heard the story of Briar Rose came to the palace and tried to break through the thorny hedge. But the thorns scratched cruelly, and seemed to grow back as quickly as they were broken off. The young men gave up, and soon no one came to the palace anymore.

In the ninety-ninth year, however, an especially brave prince came to the kingdom, and met an old man in the square of the little village that had grown up not far from Briar Rose's palace. "And are you going to try your luck with the thorn hedge," said the old man, "like the other young fools who used to come here?"

"What thorn hedge?" asked the prince. "I have not heard of it."

"It is said," the old man told him, drawing closer, "that behind the thorn hedge that stands just west of here, there is an ancient palace, and inside the palace sleeps a beautiful princess named Briar Rose, with her parents and all their court. But no one knows whether this is true or not, for the few who have tried to cut their way through the hedge have given up. No one has tried lately," the old man added, looking slyly at the prince. "No one, I daresay, has had the courage."

"I am not afraid," said the prince. "You say this Briar Rose is very beautiful?"

The old man shrugged. "I do not know," he answered. "It is said that she is. And it is said that she is good and wise as well."

"Then," said the prince, "I will go and see her for myself."

He walked west as the old man had directed, and before long he came to the hedge, and it was as high and as thick and as treacherous as the old man had warned him it would be. Day after day he hacked at it with his sword, and day after day it scratched him and seemed to grow back again as quickly as he cut it down. But he did not give up as the others had, and by the end of the seventh day he had succeeded in making a hole just large enough for him to squeeze through. But the sun was setting by then, and he decided not to go through till morning. "For," he reasoned, "if everyone has been asleep in this palace for many years, there may be nothing inside with which to make a light; I would like to be able to see the princess and also whatever danger it is that I may still be faced with." The prince piled cut thorn branches in front of the hole he had made, and spent the night guarding it restlessly.

The next day dawned clear and beautiful, and the prince yawned and stretched, and pulled aside the pile of thorn branches—and lo! as he did, the thorns on the hedge vanished and in their place grew large and beautiful flowers—for, unknown to the prince, this was the hundredth anniversary of Briar Rose's fifteenth birthday.

As the prince walked through the palace yard in wonder, he saw the horses asleep in the stable, and the hounds lying asleep just outside—but one hound grunted as the prince passed, and another moved her legs as if running after a rabbit in a dream. On the roof, over which flowers instead of thorns now nodded, he saw the doves with their heads under their wings—but one dove peeked out, waking, and began to preen his feathers as the prince passed through the great door of the palace. And there the prince marveled to see the flies asleep on the walls, and the cook in the kitchen with his hand out to box the scullery boy's ears (and the boy cringing in his sleep), and the maid sitting by the black hen which she had fallen asleep plucking.

The prince went further into the palace, still marveling at all he saw, and he saw the king and queen asleep on the threshold, and all around them their sleeping courtiers.

Then he went on still farther, looking into all the rooms as Briar Rose had done. At last he came to the dark hallway, and the door at the end of it, and the narrow winding staircase up into the tower.

Up he climbed, and opened the door to the little room in which Briar Rose was sleeping. She was so beautiful that at first he could not move, but he soon recovered enough to stoop down and give her a kiss. And at that moment Briar Rose opened her eyes and smiled at him.

When Briar Rose was fully awake, and the prince had told her what he knew of the spell she had been under, they went down the stairs together. The king awoke, and the queen, and the whole court, and looked at one another in great astonishment until they remembered the twelfth Wise Woman's words. Then they laughed and hugged one another, and went joyfully about their business. The horses in the courtyard stretched and flicked their tails; the hounds jumped up, barking; the rest of the doves pulled their heads out from under their wings, looked around, and flew down from the roof in search of food. The flies on the walls shook out their wings and buzzed; the fire in the kitchen rose up, flickering, and finished cooking the roast, which turned on its spit again and sizzled. The cook gave the boy such a box on the ear that he yelped, and the maid finished plucking the black hen as if nothing at all had happened.

And not so very long from that day, there was another splendid feast at the palace: the marriage feast of Briar Rose and her prince, both of whom afterward lived happily to the end of their days.

THUMBLING

A CERTAIN peasant and his wife were very happy together and had a comfortable life, although they were by no means wealthy. By day the man worked in the fields or cut wood, while his wife swept and baked and washed, and tended their small vegetable plot and their chickens. By night they sat cozily by the fire and dozed and talked; sometimes the husband mended boots and harnesses and sharpened tools, and the wife spun or wove or sewed. Yes, a comfortable life, indeed, and a happy one—but for one thing.

"Our house is so very quiet!" the husband said one evening when they had come home from visiting a neighbor. "Did you notice what a merry sound our neighbor's children made, laughing and whispering and tumbling over one another like so many puppies?"

"Yes," said his wife, "it is true. If only we had even one child to keep us company! It would not matter even if it were as small as my thumb, I would still love it just as much."

"Ah, well," said the man, "since we have not been blessed with a child all these years, I suppose we will not have one now."

But, happily, he was wrong, and in time they did have a child—a fine boy, only he was as small as the wife's thumb, as she had said.

"But of course he will grow," said the proud father, carefully holding his tiny son in one hand.

"Of course," said the wife—but in her heart she was not sure.

They named the baby Thumbling, and the husband made him a tiny cradle and a tiny chest to keep his clothes in, and as he grew older, the wife sewed him tiny jackets and trousers and shirts, and the husband made him tiny boots from scraps of leather. Thumbling had as much appetite as any creature his size, and ate heartily from the buttons that were his plates and the flattened acorn tops that were his bowls and drank from the hollow glass bead, one end filled, that was his cup. But he never grew.

"No matter," said his parents, "we love you just as much as we would if you were bigger. Maybe more."

Thumbling was a clever child, and easily made up games to play, swinging on grass blades and making friends of beetles, and sailing shreds of bark in puddles. But as he grew older, he longed for real adventure, and wanted to help his father the way he had seen other boys his age doing. And so one day when his father was preparing to go out and cut wood, and was complaining that all day he would have to tend the horse and cart as well as wield his axe, Thumbling jumped onto his shoulder and said, "Father, I have a plan! You will not have to watch the horse and cart all day."

"Oh?" said the father fondly, turning his head so he could see his tiny son. "And what is your plan?"

"Well," said Thumbling, "I will wait till noontime, when you will be ready to load wood. And then, if Mother will hitch Grayling to the cart, I will sit in his ear and tell him which way to go, and so bring him and the cart to you."

"What a good idea, Thumbling," said his father, patting his tiny son ever so gently with the tip of his finger. "We will try. And if it works, why then we will find other ways for you to help me. We shall be a fine team, you and I!"

So the father went off to the forest, and Thumbling looked for beetles in the vegetable garden until noontime came. Then his mother hitched up Grayling, and lifted Thumbling to his head and said, "Now, my child, do be careful! Hold on firmly so that you do not fall off—and be careful when Grayling twitches his ears to keep the flies off, for if you are not holding tightly, you could easily fall—and what then, for who would be able to find you?"

"Oh, Mother," said Thumbling, "do not worry—I will hold on and nothing will happen." And with that, Thumbling kissed his mother's knuckle and said into the horse's ear, "Gee up, Grayling."

All the way to the forest he hummed to soothe the horse and to take his own mind off the flies which buzzed around Grayling's head. Once in a while he stopped humming to say, "Now then, Grayling, to the left here," and he would say that in Grayling's left ear and make a little jump, so that the horse would feel a bit more weight on that side, like the pulling of reins. Then when they had to go to the right, he would run around to that side, holding tightly to Grayling's long hairs as he did so and pulling himself along as if clinging to ropes on shipboard. Then he would say, "Now, Grayling, to the right," and jump a little again. And this method worked so well that before the sun had left its noontime position overhead, they had reached the forest.

They had almost come up to Thumbling's father when they met two men walking toward them down the road. Oho, thought Thumbling, now we will have some fun. "Gee up!" he said to Grayling, who began to trot.

"Look," said one of the two men, "there is a driverless horse!"

"Not driverless," said the other man—for just then Thumbling shouted "Whoa!" and Grayling stopped—"but with an invisible driver who can be heard but not seen. What a marvel!"

"That cannot be," said the first man. "Let us see about that." And he peered into the cart and all around, but he could not find Thumbling.

"Gee up!" cried Thumbling, and the man stepped back in alarm as Grayling moved forward. Then he said, "Now, Grayling, to the left."

"Let us follow!" cried the second man, "for an invisible driver who directs his horse by voice alone is truly a wonder." And so they followed Thumbling and Grayling to where Thumbling's father was.

"Hello, Father!" Thumbling called when they arrived. "Here we are!"

"Here you are, indeed," said the father, reaching up so Thumbling could hop onto his hand. "Just on time, too; good lad, Thumbling—I was just finishing. Did you have any adventures along the way?"

"No," said Thumbling, "except two men thought I was invisible—see, here they come."

And the two men approached, and saw little Thumbling on his father's hand, and marveled at him.

"Do you mean," said one, "that this little man directed the horse on his way?"

"Yes, indeed," said the proud father. "He is clever for one so tiny, is he not? And he can go where we great fellows cannot, which is most useful."

"It must be," said the other man, and he looked at his companion and his companion looked at him, and a nod passed between them, for they both thought of the money they could earn if they showed Thumbling on market day as a curiosity. "My good man," said the first of the two, "we will buy this little fellow from you, and we shall treat him well."

"Not on your life!" said the father, horrified. "Not for all the gold in the world—for he is my own son, and I would not part with him."

"We will pay *very* well," said the second man, and he drew out a pouch filled with gold coins. Then he and his companion walked a little distance away so Thumbling and his father could discuss what to do.

"Father," said Thumbling, hopping up to his father's shoulder so he could whisper in his ear, "take their gold—it will make your fortune. Do not worry—I will soon find a way to come home to you."

But the father shook his head.

"Truly," said Thumbling. "I long to see the world, and this is a way I can do so and also do something for you and Mother. Just think—with that gold you will never have to scramble and scratch for a living again."

After more words in this vein, Thumbling at last won his father to his point of view. "Very well," the father said at last, and he went to the two men and said he would give them his son in exchange for the gold in the pouch. "But come back quickly," he whispered to his son before he handed him to the men. "And be careful."

"I will, Father," Thumbling promised, and then the first man put Thumbling on the brim of his hat, near a feather that was fastened there as a decoration—and off they went.

"Perhaps," said the man, as they walked down the forest road, "you would be better off in my pocket; it is chilly up there, is it not?"

"Oh, no," said Thumbling. "I like fresh air. And besides, when the wind blows, I can shelter myself behind this wonderful feather."

So on the two men walked, and Thumbling had a fine time looking out at all they passed—for soon they came out of the forest onto a wider road, and there were fields and cows and farmhouses to look at, and once in a while, a passing carter with his horse.

But as dusk began to fall, Thumbling wondered how he would find his way home after all, so again he thought of a plan. He waited for a gust of wind and then he shouted, "Oh, sir, the tip of your wonderful feather has blown off—put me down quickly so that I can get it for you!"

So the man lifted Thumbling down, for he was vain about the feather—and no sooner was he on the ground than Thumbling ran behind a small rock, and then darted into a mousehole.

"Where are you?" called the man. "I cannot see you in the twilight. Do you have my feather yet?"

"Not yet," called Thumbling from the entrance to the mousehole, making his voice sound thin and far away. "I am just chasing it. . . ."

"Your feather looks fine to me," said the other man, examining his friend's hat. "I do not see that any of it is missing."

So the first man took his hat off, and looked and saw that the feather was indeed just as it had always been, and then he knew that he had been tricked. But neither man could find Thumbling, nor did they know where his father lived, so there was nothing they could do but go on their way grumbling.

"Thank you, friend mouse," Thumbling said, when the men had gone and Thumbling had explained why he had gone uninvited into the mouse's home—and then he left.

He walked for a while and then as the dusk thickened into night, he began searching in the grass and among the flowering weeds for someplace to spend the night. An animal's hole will not do, he thought, because of the animal, and I cannot climb a tree, although if I could I might find a safe hole or an abandoned nest. And I dare not wrap myself in a leaf and lie upon a bit of moss, for who knows what might come along and step on me? And I cannot—ah, but here is the very thing! And indeed he had found the very thing, for right in his path was an empty snail shell, bleached white and clean by the sun. Thumbling rolled it into the shelter of a large rock and crawled down the shell's twisty front hall to the large, round room at its end. And here he curled himself up and fell asleep.

It was still night when voices woke him. "We have time left," said one, seeming to put something heavy down, "to go to the pastor's house—the rich pastor, I mean; the one who has the silver and gold plates."

"Yes," said the other voice, "we still have time, but we have no way of getting into the pastor's house. He has bars on his windows, I'm told, and a large dog, and no one has been able to rob him yet."

Oho, thought Thumbling, here is a good game! And out loud he said, "Poo—bars on windows are no trouble to me; I could get you the silver plates and golden platters with no trouble at all!"

"Who was that?" said the first robber—for, of course, robbers they were, and the heavy sound Thumbling had heard was a bag full of jewels that they had already stolen that night.

"Where are you?" cried the other robber. "Perhaps we can join forces, if you are so clever."

"I am right here," shouted Thumbling, "under your very noses."

"I do not believe this," whispered the other robber, growing pale with fright, "but I think it is this snail shell that has spoken."

"Look more closely!" shouted Thumbling, stepping out of the shell.

And the robbers bent down and saw the tiny youth standing there, hands on his hips, smiling at them.

"You see," said Thumbling, "I can go where you cannot; I can slip through the bars on those windows you were talking about, and slip the silver plates and golden platters through them out to you."

"How will you move them?" asked one robber doubtfully. "You are so very small."

"Plates are round," said Thumbling, "and platters are nearly so; anything I can roll, I can move."

The two robbers looked at each other and shrugged their shoulders and then nodded their heads. "Very well," one said, "come along." And he scooped Thumbling up, and put him in his pocket.

When they got to the pastor's house, the robber took Thumbling out and put him on the windowsill, and Thumbling passed easily through the bars. "Now to have some fun," he said to himself. Taking a deep breath, he shouted as loudly as he could, "Now then! Do you want everything that is here, friends, or is it just one or two special things you are after?"

"Hush," cried the robbers in alarm. "Softly, lest you wake someone!"

"What?" shouted Thumbling. "I cannot hear you!"

"But everyone can hear *you*," said one of the robbers in a loud whisper. "*Will* you be silent?"

"Take everything," said the other robber, his face close to the window, "only do it *quietly*."

"Hahahah," laughed Thumbling and then called, "I still cannot hear you; what is it you wanted me to STEAL?"

And at that the pastor's dog woke up and barked, waking the pastor.

"Quickly," said the robbers, hearing the dog, "just pass anything out—quickly—do hurry!" They held the open bag under the window.

"What?" shouted Thumbling again. "You say you want one of the golden platters first? Or did you say one of the silver plates? They are rather nice—a pretty pattern."

"Here, here!" cried a new voice—and the pastor, in his nightshirt and with his dog, burst out of the house and chased the robbers away. While that was going on, Thumbling quietly withdrew to the barn, where he made himself a nest in some hay, telling himself he would worry about finding his way home when morning came.

But in the morning, the pastor's milkmaid came out to milk the cows, and she picked up the very pile of hay Thumbling was in and fed it to a large brown and white cow.

"Wait, stop!" Thumbling cried as he felt himself slipping down the cow's throat—but it was too late and he was soon stuck inside.

What a dark room, he thought, looking around, and there are far too many deliveries, he thought, as more hay came sliding down the cow's throat to join him in the stomach. "No more, no more!" Thumbling cried, dodging the hay, "for there will soon be no room for me!"

Meanwhile, the maid was milking the selfsame cow, and heard Thumbling cry out. Thinking it was the cow that spoke, she ran to her master in a great fright. "The brown and white cow is bewitched!" she cried, "and just now spoke to me!" So the pastor, who was now dressed and wanting his breakfast, ran with her to the barn. And just as they arrived Thumbling called out, "Stop—stop—no more hay!"

"The Devil must have her!" the pastor said, and he ordered the cow killed, and her stomach thrown on the trash heap.

As soon as Thumbling realized what had happened, he tried his best to escape, but before he could find a way out, a wolf came by and, seeing the stomach, swallowed it whole.

My, my, thought Thumbling, now I really do need a plan—but wolves are greedy animals, so perhaps there is a way out of this, and home, too. "Sir wolf!" he cried aloud, "are you not still hungry?"

"Yes," answered the wolf, "I am indeed. But who are you?"

"I thought you were hungry," said Thumbling, "for I am your stomach and I know about these things; I am, in fact, quite empty. Now listen carefully: I know a house where you can find a true feast."

"Just what I want, stomach," said the wolf. "Where might it be?"

"Do you know the road that runs past the pastor's house and into a forest where peasants sometimes cut wood?" asked Thumbling.

"Why, yes," said the wolf. "I know it well."

"Then go south along it," said Thumbling, "and into the forest. Turn right and left and right and left on the forest road till you come to a peasant's cottage with a vegetable garden in front. But do not bother with that; go into the house through the hole you will find under the kitchen sink. In the kitchen there are meat and bread and cakes and all manner of good things, fit for a king."

"I will go there at once," said the wolf, and he began to run.

He got to Thumbling's father's house—for, of course, that is where Thumbling had directed him—when it was still daylight, and so lay down at the edge of the forest to wait till it was dark. As soon as night fell, the wolf crept to the little house and waited till all was quiet while poor Thumbling had to stay inside him, hoping and hoping that the wolf had found the right house and that all would go as he had planned. "What are the people doing now, wolf?" he asked when he could stand it no longer. "Look in the window and tell me."

So the wolf climbed up and looked in the window and then got down again lest he be seen and said, "An old man is sitting by the fire mending boots; and an old woman is spinning, and they are saying that they miss their son, who went away with two men in exchange for a pouch of gold. What odd creatures humans are!"

"Yes," said Thumbling, his heart leaping with joy, "they are odd indeed."

When at last the fire in the little house had been banked and the man and woman had gone to bed, the wolf crept through the hole under the sink and feasted on all he could find, and smacked his lips and said it was good. And then when he could eat no more, he tried to squeeze out the hole under the sink—but now, as Thumbling had hoped, he was too big because of all he had eaten. Now Thumbling, who had put a large cabbage between himself and the other food the wolf had swallowed, shouted,

"Why, what is this, friend wolf? Are you stuck? Hahahah—that comes of being so greedy! Now what will you do?"

"Hush," said the wolf in alarm. "Be quiet—you will wake the people of the house and they will catch me here!"

"And a good thing, too," shouted Thumbling. "You are such a greedy beast!" And he went on yelling and shouting until his parents woke up and came into the kitchen and found the wolf.

"Wait," said Thumbling's father, thrusting his wife back into the other room, "we will get the axe and the scythe. Then we will creep up on him, and I will hit him first with the axe. If he needs another blow, you be ready with the scythe." So they fetched the tools, but when they came back with them, Thumbling cried, "Father! Mother! Be careful how you swing, for I am here, in the wolf's stomach!"

The parents were astonished, but overjoyed, and they set about their job most carefully, and soon had killed the wolf and taken Thumbling out.

"Thumbling!" they both cried in joy, embracing him carefully, "are you all right?"

"Yes, indeed," said Thumbling. "I am fine and I have seen the world from the brim of a hat, from a mousehole and a snail shell and a robber's pocket, from behind the bars on a pastor's window, and lastly from a cow's stomach and a wolf's, neither of which did I like at all. And now that I have seen the world, I am happy to be home and glad to settle down, where we can live in peace and do our work and have the gold of those two foolish men with which to guard against hard times!"

So at that the father kissed Thumbling and brought him a fresh, clean suit of clothes. And the wife set out Thumbling's little plates and bowls and his glass bead mug, and they all three feasted on what the wolf had left them, and though it was little it seemed like great plenty, for they were so happy to be together once again. And together they remained for many years to come.

THE GOLDEN BIRD

In the days when the world was full of marvels, and kings and queens were commonplace, there were in a certain kingdom three brothers, who were princes. The two oldest were cut of one cloth, as you will see, but the third was not like them.

Now the king their father had a splendid orchard, most of whose trees bore juicy red apples, but the best tree of all bore golden ones. This tree was so special that the king counted its fruit every morning to make sure no one had stolen any during the night. Year after year he did this, and year after year there were always as many apples as he expected.

But after many years, a morning came when the king counted his golden apples, and there were ninety-nine instead of the hundred there had been the morning before. In astonishment he counted again, and there were still only ninety-nine. So he went to his oldest son and said, "Guard my apples tonight, and tell me if anyone is stealing them. Take care that you do not sleep even for a moment, for who knows what manner of creature might be the thief."

But when no one had come by midnight, the eldest son was sure that no one would come, and allowed his eyes to close. And the next morning, there were ninety-eight apples.

So that night, the king ordered his middle son to watch, and he said the same thing to him that he had said to his eldest son. But the middle son also felt drowsy at midnight and, like his brother, was sure no one would come that late, and so allowed himself to sleep. And the next morning, there were only ninety-seven golden apples.

"This must stop," said the king, and he sent for his youngest son, and gave him the same orders. "Though since his brothers have failed," the king said to himself, "he may well, also, for he has never seemed as bright as they."

But this son was in fact by no means stupid, and he was also determined to do what his brothers had not done, and so he stayed awake. At midnight he did feel sleepy, but he walked up and down until his eyes no longer felt so heavy, and was able to shake sleep off. And just as he had recovered himself, he felt a wind and then he saw something moving, as if a bit of sunlight had come down from the nighttime sky and was flying toward him—but it was a golden bird with long, golden feathers of great and dazzling beauty. As the young prince drew his bow, the bird perched on a limb of the tree and began to reach for an apple with its beak. The prince let go his arrow, but though the bird flew off, the arrow had missed it, and only one golden feather floated to the ground. The prince took this to his father and told him all that had happened.

The king sent for his treasurer who declared that the feather was worth as much as the entire kingdom and possibly the next one as well. "Then I must have the whole bird!" cried the king, "for if I do, I will be the richest king in the world!"

"I will get the bird for you, Father," said the king's eldest son, wishing to make up for his failure in the orchard and hoping that his father would reward him handsomely. And so he set out.

When he reached the next kingdom and had not yet found the bird, he met a fox sitting beside a well just off the road. He pointed his gun at the fox and was about to shoot when the fox said, "Do not shoot, my friend, for I know what you seek and can help you."

"Oh?" said the prince. "And how might you be able to do that?"

"Put your gun away," said the fox, "and I will tell you."

So the prince put his gun away and sat down on a stone, and listened.

"I know," said the fox, "that you seek the golden bird—is this not so?"

"Why, yes," said the prince, surprised, "but how do you know that?"

"I have my ways," said the fox. "Now, listen. Not far from here, but still in this same kingdom, there is a village. In the village two inns stand next to each other. One is bright and rich and merry and there are always people inside singing and dancing and feasting. The other inn is poor and dark and dingy, and looks deserted. Go to that village, and when evening falls, take a room at the dull inn, not the other."

"How will that help me?" asked the prince, thinking that the fox spoke foolishly—for why go into a dull inn when a merry one is nearby?

"That I cannot say," answered the fox. "But do as I advise and you will see."

"Perhaps you cannot say because you do not know," said the prince. "You are trying to trick me! Be off with you lest I shoot after all." And he made as if to aim at the fox, who ran into the woods, his tail streaming behind him.

The prince walked on, and by evening he had come to the village, and all was as the fox had described. "What nonsense," said the prince to himself, viewing the poor inn with distaste—and he turned to the rich one, and went inside. And once in, he was caught in an endless web of merry-making, and he forgot all about the golden bird and spent his days in empty jollity.

Now the king his father watched every day from a high tower in hope that his son would soon return with the golden bird, but his vigil was never rewarded. At last the middle son said, "Father, some ill is sure to have befallen my brother; I will go in search of him and of the bird, too. Before long, I will bring both back to you."

"Very well," said the king, "but keep your wits about you."

"I will, Father," the middle prince promised, and he went on his way.

It was not long before he, too, passed into the next kingdom and met the same fox his brother had met, and received the same advice. How silly, thought the middle prince when the fox had spoken, and he, too, made as if to shoot, and the fox ran off. How silly, he thought again when he came to the two inns. And soon he joined his brother in the merry one, where all that looked bright was truly shabby in the end.

Soon the king began again to watch from his high tower, and again his vigil was not rewarded. At last his youngest son went to him and said, "Father, I will now go forth and find my brothers, and perhaps your golden bird as well."

"You cannot go," said the king. "You have even less sense than your brothers."

"Then my loss will not be so great if I do not return," said the youngest prince, and off he went.

He traveled the same road as his brothers, and in the next kingdom met the same fox, but instead of holding his gun up to shoot, he said, "Hello, friend fox; do not be afraid," and he held out his hand in friendly fashion.

"What a kind young man!" said the fox. "And are you, too, seeking the golden bird?"

"Why, yes," said the prince in surprise. "Do you know my brothers?"

"Possibly," said the fox, "but I tell you what: Go on to the village that is below here, and you will find two inns." And he gave the youngest prince the same advice he had given his brothers. But this time, since the youngest prince had not tried to shoot him, the fox gave him a ride to the village on his back, and put him down in front of the two inns. Without even looking at the merry one, the prince went into the other, where he had a wholesome meal and spent a quiet night.

In the morning, he met the fox again outside the village. "I see you know how to take advice," said the fox, "and so I will tell you what you want to know—but do all that I say carefully, or it will come to naught.

This road leads to the castle that guards the next kingdom from this one. You will find the guardsmen all asleep, and if you let them lie undisturbed, they will be no trouble to you. Go into the castle and search till you come to a room that is empty but for two cages. One cage is golden and very beautiful; the other is plain wood, but in it is the bird you want. Take the bird in its wooden cage; do not put it in the golden one, no matter how much you think it more suitable. If you do this, all will be well."

The prince agreed, and so the fox let him climb on his back and ran so quickly along the road it was as if they were flying. And at last they came to the castle that guarded the next kingdom, and the fox left.

The young prince stepped over the sleeping guardsmen and went from room to room inside the castle, ignoring the purple hangings and the rich furnishings and all the gold and silver ornaments, set about with jewels. At last he came to a bare room—bare except for the two cages the fox had described. And there in the plain wooden cage was the beautiful golden bird, preening its long, golden feathers, and on the floor of the wooden cage were three golden apples from his father's tree.

But the wooden cage looked shabby in comparison to the golden bird and the golden apples. "How can I take this bird to my father in such an ugly wooden cage?" the prince said to himself—and so he reached into the wooden cage to seize the bird and put it in the other. But as soon as the bird was outside the cage it opened its beak and called out shrilly, waking the guard, who came in and took the prince away to prison.

The next morning the prince was led into the throne room of the king of that region, and he told his story in front of ten judges. The judges wanted to sentence him to death for trying to take the golden bird, but the king thought he should be given another chance because he was so young. So it was arranged that the prince could live if he went on to the next kingdom and brought the king a certain golden horse that he said was his, but had been stolen. This horse could run faster than any creature on earth. "And if you bring him to me," said the king, "your life will be your own

again, and you may also have the golden bird as your reward."

So the prince thanked the king for his mercy and left, but he walked slowly, for no one had told him where the road to the next kingdom lay. Just as he was about to give up hope, he met the fox again.

"You foolish boy," said the fox. "Do you see what not taking my advice has done to you? You did not heed me, and look at the trouble that follows you now."

"I know," said the prince sadly. "You are right; I was foolish."

"Well, well," said the fox, "perhaps you have learned your lesson; you at least chose the right inn to stay at. Jump on my back, and I will take you to the next kingdom, and to the stable where the golden horse lives." The prince climbed on the fox's back and off they flew.

When they got to the stable, the fox whispered, "See how the stablemen are sleeping? Do not wake them and all will be well with you. Go inside quietly, saddle the golden horse, and lead him out. But heed this: There are two saddles, and the one you must put on the horse is made of wood and leather."

The fox then went away, and the prince crept quietly into the stable where, sure enough, was a beautiful golden horse the likes of which the prince had never seen.

The prince reached for the saddle of wood and leather that hung near the horse's stall, but then he saw the other, and it was made of burnished gold, and studded with precious stones that matched the beautiful horse's eyes. "This saddle is clearly meant for this horse," the prince said to himself. "It is the same colors as he. And besides, how could I possibly return this horse to a king with a poor, plain saddle when there is a rich one waiting?" And so the prince lifted the golden saddle down but as soon as it so much as brushed against the horse's back, the horse whinnied loudly and woke the stablemen, who ran in shouting, "Stop thief!" and took the prince off to the prison in the king's palace.

The next morning the prince was brought before the king and his judges, and again the judges had one idea but the king another. "You may live," said the king at last, "if you will rescue the beautiful princess who is locked inside the golden castle that lies beyond here in the next kingdom. And if you bring her to me you may have the golden horse as your reward, along with your life."

Again the prince had no idea what road to take, and he walked dejectedly along until, just as he was wishing he would meet the fox again, the fox appeared. "I should ignore you," the fox said angrily, "for you are being ridiculously stubborn, but again, you showed good sense about the inns, so there must be some in you. Heed what I say: This road leads into the next kingdom, and to the castle you seek; the princess is inside it. She comes out only once each day, to go to the bathing house. All you need do is wait till she goes to the bathing-house door, and then run up to her and ask her to go with you. She will go as long as you do not allow her to say good-bye to anyone. If you let her do that, all will come to naught, and you will be in great danger, as before." And the fox took the prince upon his back and carried him to the golden castle, and left him there.

The prince waited till evening and at last the princess, who was most beautiful indeed, came out and walked slowly to the bathing house. When she reached its door, the prince ran up to her and said, "Will you come with me, lovely princess? A noble king wants to see you."

"I will," said the princess, "but I must first say good-bye to those here who will miss me."

"No," said the prince, "you may not; I dare not let you do it. Just come, and all will be well."

"But I must!" cried the princess, and she began to weep and pleaded so piteously that the prince at last gave in. "Very well," he said, "only be quick—and do not wake the guards."

And so the princess ran into the castle, and within minutes the guards came and seized the prince and put him again in prison.

"You must die," said the king the next morning, "for this deed—unless you can flatten the hill that blocks the view from my window. If you do that in a week and a day, you can go free, and I will give you the princess's hand in marriage as your reward."

So the prince went outside, under guard, and he dug all that day and all the next, and he dug as long as he could after nightfall, but the hill was almost as high as it had been when he had started. The week soon passed and when only the day was left, the prince was in despair because he could tell even without looking that the hill still blocked the king's view.

On the evening of the seventh day the fox appeared at his elbow as he was digging and said, "You poor fool; you cannot listen, can you? And yet this time you tried to do as I said and only went against my advice out of pity for the princess when she wept. Well, well, I will help you once more. Go to sleep, and I will finish digging."

So the prince went to sleep, too exhausted to worry about how the fox was going to do in one night what he himself had not been able to do in a week—but when he woke, the hill was gone and the sun was shining brightly.

The prince went before the king of that kingdom and his judges and when they all looked outside they were able to see across the distant hills and beyond. So the king sent for the princess who had been in the other castle and gave her to the prince in marriage as he had promised. After the wedding feast, the prince and his new bride set out to return to the prince's kingdom.

In a while they again met the fox, who sat before the prince and said, "Now you are improving! But you still do not have what you set out for."

"No," said the prince, "and I know not how to get it."

"You must do this first," said the fox, while the princess patted his head and rubbed his ears. "You must take your bride to the king who asked you to rescue her, as you would have, had you been successful. And because he will be so glad to see her, he will give you anything you want.

You must ask him for the golden horse, which he will give to you, and as soon as the horse is brought to you, you must mount him. Then you must say good-bye to all in that palace, and anyone whom you wish to have go with you, you must give your hand to, and if that person wishes to go, you will be able to pull them onto the horse and ride off."

"I do not understand," said the prince, turning to his bride, "why I must take you to the king who asked for you when you so willingly married me."

"Because," she said, "that king is not my suitor but my father."

"But who," asked the prince, astonished, "was the king who gave you to me in marriage, and at whose castle you were living?"

"That king is my uncle," said the princess. "He took me from my father when I was an infant, for he had no children."

"Alas," said the prince, "if he is your father and you have not seen him for many years, you will perhaps want to stay with him."

"That will be as it will be," said the princess serenely, still stroking the fox, and that was all she would say.

Then they took leave of the fox and walked back to the kingdom of the princess's father, and because they were on foot, it was some time before they arrived. Along the way they talked and found that they liked many of the same things. When they arrived at the princess's father's castle, there was great rejoicing, and her true father gladly gave the prince the golden horse—"For," he said, "you have brought my daughter back to me and provided me with a son as well; I am glad she has such a fine husband." When the prince was ready to leave, he mounted the golden horse and stretched his hand down to the princess. Smiling, she took it, and off they rode as swiftly as the wind, faster than any creature on earth.

In time they again met the fox, who said to the prince, "Better and better; you are improving markedly." After the princess had slid down from the golden horse and patted the fox and whispered in his ear, the fox said to the prince, "But tell me, do you yet have what you set out for?"

"No," said the prince, "for I do not yet have the golden bird or my two brothers; although you have led me to the golden horse, you have not led me to them."

"Well," said the fox, "now you must do this: You must go back to the castle of the golden bird. You must ride there on the golden horse, for it is there that you were asked to get that noble steed. The people there will be overjoyed to see him for he was stolen from there by the king in whose stable you found him. Ask for the golden bird while the people are still rejoicing and it will be brought to you, and if the horse wishes to stay he will stay, and if he wishes to go with you, he will let you mount him. You must leave the princess with me."

This was hard for the prince, but the princess urged him to heed the fox, and so soon they parted and he rode back alone. When he got to the castle of the golden bird there was much rejoicing as soon as the people there saw the golden horse. The king gave the prince the golden bird, for he was so glad to see that the horse was well. Then, with the bird in its cage, the prince turned and mounted the golden horse easily, and the people and their king, seeing that the horse wished to stay with the prince and that the prince treated him well, let the horse go.

Soon the fox appeared again, bringing the princess back to the prince. She had braided flowers together and made a garland for him, and another for the fox. "Perfect," said the fox to the prince, "or nearly so. You now have your bird and you may soon find your brothers. But beware, for not all that you think you want now will you truly want in the end. Remember this: Do not buy any man. And remember this: Be careful of open wells; never sit on the edge of one to rest. And now," the fox went on, with the princess standing by his side, "since I have done so much for you, I must ask you to do something for me."

"What is that?" asked the prince.

"You must shoot me," said the fox, "and then you must cut off my head and my feet."

"I cannot do that," cried the prince. "What thanks would that be for all you have done for me?"

"It would be great thanks," the fox said, "though I cannot tell you why."

"I cannot do it," said the prince.

"Very well," said the fox sadly, "and so we must part." And he ran off into the woods—and the princess wept to see him go as she mounted the golden horse behind the prince.

"A remarkable beast," the prince said to his bride as they rode on. "And what a strange request he made."

But the princess made no answer, and when the prince turned around he saw that she was weeping still, so he comforted her as best he could, and they rode on.

Soon they came again to the village in which the prince had stayed at the humble inn, and the streets were so full of people that he could not pass through. "Some great event must be about to occur," he said to the princess, and then he asked a farmer what was going forward.

"Oh," said the farmer, "why, sir, a hanging, to be sure—two men who have spent these last months in merrymaking and squandered all their money. Once their money was gone, they stole from others, you see, and did all manner of evil deeds, one deed leading to the next. There they are now, mounting the gallows."

The prince looked and to his horror saw his two brothers.

"Can no one save them?" he asked.

"Bless you, no," said the farmer, "unless someone wishes to buy them—to pay for their lives, that is—but they are so wicked, no one will do that."

"I will," cried the prince, forgetting the fox's warning, "for they are my brothers," and he went to the magistrate and did so.

So now the two older brothers traveled with the young prince and his bride and the golden horse and the golden bird. And they knew not which they wanted more: the bird or the horse or their brother's bride.

In time they all came to the part of the road where each had met the fox by the well, and since they were thirsty and tired they decided to stop there awhile. The two older brothers began to recount their adventures and while they did so, the younger forgot the fox's second warning and sat down at the edge of the well—whereupon the two older brothers pushed him into it and rode off on the golden horse, taking the golden bird and the princess with them. "Do not speak of what has just happened," they told the weeping princess, "or we will kill you. You will be cared for—in time, one of us will marry you. Meanwhile, remain silent if you value your life."

It was not a long journey from there to their father's palace in comparison to the distance they had come, and when they arrived the king was full of great joy when he saw not only his two older sons and the golden bird he had wished for but also a golden horse and a lovely princess as well. But despite the rejoicing all around them in the palace, those three remained sad. The princess did nothing but weep, and the bird never sang, and the horse stood in his stall all day with drooping head and he would touch neither oats nor hay nor bran.

As to the youngest brother, the two older said nothing, but they were sure he was dead. This, however, was not so, for the well had gone dry and had a thick carpet of moss at its bottom, so the prince had only been stunned when he fell.

When he had recovered his senses and climbed out again, there was the fox sitting by the well, shaking his head. "You are back to your old ways," he said. "You did the two very things I warned you against."

"I know," said the prince, hanging his head, "but perhaps I have learned now."

"Then hear me," said the fox, "for your brothers think you are dead, and would do you great evil if they learned otherwise. Go home to your father's palace but not as yourself. Disguise yourself well, or it will go badly with you."

So the prince changed clothes with a beggar, and went home to his father's palace, where, in truth, no one recognized him. But, miraculously, as soon as he had crossed the moat, the golden bird began to sing most beautifully, and the golden horse ate all his oats and raised his head and whinnied to be let out of his stall into the sun, and the princess stopped weeping and smiled as she went cheerfully about the palace. "What is this?" asked the king. "Why are you now so happy when you have been so sad?"

"I know not," answered the princess, "but I feel great joy, as if my true love had come for me."

"Your true love!" exclaimed the king in amazement. "But I thought one of my two older sons was going to marry you."

"No," said the princess, surprising him still more, "for I am married already." And she felt so sure her husband was alive she told the king all that had happened.

When he had heard the true story, the king held back his anger for a time and sent his servants throughout the palace and into the orchard and the garden, and around the courtyard and into the stables, and had every person there brought into the great hall. Among the people in the courtyard whom they knew, the servants found a strange beggar and brought him in as well. When everyone was in the great hall, the king said to the princess, "Is your true love here?" and the princess looked and soon recognized her husband despite his beggar's clothes. "Yes," she cried, running to him and embracing him. "This is my true love—your youngest son, your majesty." At that the two older sons trembled, and well they might, for the king let his anger go and bellowed his rage at them, and ordered them to be thrown into the dungeon to be punished.

That very evening, as the prince and princess were walking in the king's orchard, the fox appeared, weeping, under the tree with the golden apples. "What is it, friend fox?" cried the prince, going down on one knee. "What is it that makes you weep on a day when all are so happy?"

"I still have one wish," said the fox, "as you very well know, and I cannot be happy till it is granted."

"What wish is that?" asked the prince—but he knew already, and feared it.

"You remember well," said the fox. "It is that you kill me and cut off my head and feet."

The prince shuddered, but the princess, laying her hand tenderly on the fox's head, said, "Do as he wishes, my husband; do it for my sake if not for his."

"Would you have me be so hard-hearted? Would you be so yourself?" asked the prince.

"Nay, husband; have faith and do what the fox says. He has never yet been wrong and he is not wrong now."

So the prince, with much reluctance, did what the fox had asked, and no sooner had he done so than the fox became a man, who embraced the princess joyfully, telling the prince that he was her brother, and had been changed to a fox long ago when he had tried to rescue her from their uncle.

Now all was well again in the kingdom of the golden apples, and all was well in the kingdom of the golden bird, and of the golden horse, and of the princess, and in the village also. And all remained peaceful until the next adventure began.

CINDERELLA

There once was an ordinary man who was rich and lived in a great house with his wife and only daughter, and the daughter and mother were as close as if they were friends or sisters. But one day the mother fell gravely ill and, as she knew she would soon die, she sent for her child and said to her tenderly, "Do not grieve for me too bitterly, my little one, for I will always watch over you, and the birds of the forest will protect you." Soon after that she died, and the girl wept many bitter tears.

Although a year went by, the girl still went faithfully every day to her mother's grave, as did the birds of the forest, who comforted her. One day a great sadness came upon her, for her father had taken another wife, a greedy, cold woman, who wanted all his wealth for herself and her two daughters. These two daughters were beautiful to look at, but they were as greedy as their mother, and they laughed at their stepsister for her gentleness and for the love she had for the birds of the forest. They, too, wanted all the father's wealth for themselves and were jealous of his own daughter's beauty. Because the father was often away and could not watch over his household himself, the stepsisters and stepmother told him that his own daughter had become willful and bad, and urged him to let them punish her. At first he did not believe them, but since his own daughter merely hung her head when they accused her and did not defend herself, he at last agreed. So the poor girl was given an ugly old dress to wear and made to work in the kitchen. From that day on she was treated in all ways like the lowest of servants, and soon it was as if she had never been the daughter of the house. Because her stepsisters often teased her by emptying bowls of peas or lentils into the ashes and making her pick them out, she was often covered with cinders and soot—so they called her Cinderella.

But Cinderella still went every day to her mother's grave, where the birds of the forest sang to her and comforted her, and listened as she told them everything that had happened to her.

One day, when the father had to go on a longer journey than usual, he asked his stepdaughters what presents he might bring them on his return. "Oh," said the older, "two beautiful dresses, made of silk with rich embroidery."

"Jewels," said the other, "as many as you can carry, and pure white pearls."

"And what about you, Cinderella?" the father asked sorrowfully—for it still pained his heart to think that his own daughter was as bad and as lazy as he was constantly told she was. "If you are very good, I will bring you something, too. What would you like?"

"Nothing so costly as my stepsisters wish for," said Cinderella. "But if when you are riding home again, a branch brushes against your head, why, bring me that, and I will be well content."

At this, Cinderella's stepsisters laughed till tears came to their eyes. "Listen to the little fool," said the older sister. "Not only is she lazy and good for nothing, but she is also stupid!"

"The stupidest girl in the kingdom," said the younger sister—and, as soon as the father had left, she took a large handful of dried lentils, which are smaller than peas, and threw them into the ashes. "Here," she said to Cinderella, "just sort these, would you? Put the good ones in a bowl, and soak them clean for soup."

Both sisters laughed, but Cinderella, without a word, went down on her knees in the ashes and began picking the lentils out and sorting them.

When in a few weeks the father came home from his journey, the two stepsisters paraded throughout the house in their new finery, but Cinderella took the little hazel twig her father had cut for her to her mother's grave and planted it. In time, watered by the rain and by her tears, it grew into a fine, leafy tree that the birds of the forest loved to sit in.

One day when Cinderella was picking lentils out of the ashes, she scraped her knee painfully upon the hearth, and when she had finished in the kitchen she went to her mother's grave and wept, saying:

Now hear my wish, my hazel tree:
I need some comfort for my knee.

And a little silver gray bird that was sitting in the hazel tree's branches flew down with one of its own feathers in its mouth and brushed the soot off Cinderella's knee and helped her clean and bandage it.

When Cinderella got back to the house that evening, her sisters were running about trying on their clothes and jewels and brushing their hair in different ways. They began shouting orders to Cinderella as soon as she came in. "Cinderella, bring my ribbons!" cried one.

"Cinderella, my pearls!" cried the other.

"My petticoat—my silver necklace—my this—my that!"

Cinderella was kept so busy running from room to room that it was some time before she learned what the fuss was about—but at last her stepmother came in and said, "You should be happy for your sisters, Cinderella. The king is giving a ball for his son, so that he can choose a bride, and he has invited only the fairest maidens in the land. Just think, a messenger came today asking for the daughters of this house to go. The feasting and dancing will last for three days, so you will have to work hard to make sure your sisters' clothes are ready each afternoon."

I am not so ugly, Cinderella thought. Why did the king not invite me? But she knew why. No one knew she existed anymore, since she worked in the kitchen all day long and was so often covered in ashes.

Then she thought more about what the invitation had said, and she summoned all her courage and went to her stepmother and said, "I am a daughter of this house. In fact, I am the only true daughter my father has; why am I not to go?"

At this the stepmother fell into fits of laughter. "You!" she cried, "why, look at you! There is a smudge on your nose and another on your cheek; your hair is covered with soot and ashes and is in tangles; your dress, such as it is, is torn, and your shoes are covered with mud. You go! Indeed!"

"Water will clean the ashes from my face and hair," said Cinderella, "and my stepsisters have plenty of dresses. I could easily borrow one of theirs."

"Ugh!" said the older stepsister. "Let you wear my clothes? Never!"

"You would look a fool dressed up," said the other stepsister. "Like a chicken in clothes, or one of your precious birds—ha! ha!"

But the father, hearing what the commotion was about, looked up from the preparations he was making for yet another journey and said mildly, "She *is* a daughter of this house."

Whereupon the stepmother sighed and said, "Very well. If she can finish her work first, she may go." At that, the father left—but when he was gone, the stepmother took a huge double handful of lentils and threw them into the kitchen fire, saying, "Pick these out and bring me a bowl filled with the good ones. If you can finish in an hour, you may go." She said that only because she was sure Cinderella would never be able to finish in that time.

Cinderella ran to her mother's grave and said:

> Now hear my wish, my hazel tree:
> I need my birds to work for me.

And the little silver gray bird flew down and led her back to the kitchen, where all the other forest birds were already assembled, picking the lentils out of the ashes with their beaks, and dropping the good ones into a bowl.

Just before the hour was up, the bowl was full and there were no more lentils on the hearth, so the silver gray bird led the other birds away. And Cinderella took the bowl to her stepmother. "Here," she said, in triumph and hope. "I have finished with the lentils."

The stepmother was startled and angry, and did not know what to do, but she was still determined to keep Cinderella from going to the ball—for she knew that Cinderella was lovelier than her own daughters. "I see, Cinderella," she said. "You have indeed done what I said, but you still cannot go to the ball. You have no clothes and you are filthy."

"You said I could go," Cinderella told her, "if I finished in an hour." And she wept so bitterly that her stepmother became vexed at the sound and, calling angrily at her to be silent, she stalked into the kitchen, filled an enormous bowl with lentils, and threw them into the ashes. "Pick these out in an hour," she said, sure that Cinderella could not, "and perhaps you may go."

So Cinderella ran again to her mother's grave and said:

Now hear my wish, my hazel tree:
I need my birds to work for me.

And the silver gray bird flew down as before and led Cinderella to the kitchen and within an hour, all the lentils were picked and sorted.

But this time when Cinderella took the lentils to her stepmother, her stepmother became even more angry and said, "Go away; I do not believe you did the task as I ordered. You may not come with us." She and Cinderella's stepsisters hurried away, for by now their coach was waiting outside to take them to the ball.

Poor Cinderella, weeping, went to her mother's grave once more and when the silver gray bird had comforted her with his singing, she said:

Now hear my wish, my hazel tree:
I need a dress to cover me.

At this the bird flew down with a beautiful gold and silver dress, and also silver dancing slippers, beautifully embroidered. Cinderella thanked the bird and quickly washed, put on the dress and the slippers and went to the ball. There, everyone stared at her as she climbed the wide staircase to the ballroom, for she was more beautiful than any other young girls there. Even her own stepsisters and stepmother admired her. They had no thought that she was Cinderella, for they had never seen her clean and dressed up before. Besides, they knew Cinderella was home in the kitchen scrubbing and cooking.

As soon as Cinderella stood inside the ballroom, the prince went up to her and asked her to dance, and from that moment on he would dance with no one else, nor would he let anyone else dance with her. Cinderella danced till she was tired, and then she danced till she was exhausted, and then she knew she should go home lest her family arrive before her. "I will take you home," said the prince, when she told him she must leave, "for I would like to see where you live and who your father is." But Cinderella was afraid that she would be badly punished if her family knew she had gone to the ball after all, so she fled down the stairs and outside so fast that the prince could not catch her.

When Cinderella's stepmother and stepsisters got home, there was Cinderella in her old, torn dress, fast asleep upon the hearth. They never suspected that she was the beautiful maiden who had taken the prince's attention away from them and every other young girl that night.

"Never mind," they comforted each other, "perhaps she will not go to the ball tomorrow, or perhaps he will not be so taken with her a second time."

The next afternoon, when her stepsisters and stepmother had left for the ball and her father was still away, Cinderella went again to her mother's grave and said:

Now hear my wish, my hazel tree:
I need a dress to cover me.

And the bird brought her another dress, more beautiful than the first one, more gold than silver this time, and another pair of beautiful dancing slippers to match. And at the ball all happened as before; everyone gasped at Cinderella's beauty, the prince most of all, and he would dance with no one else. At the end, when she wanted to go home, he again wanted to follow, but she ran from him again, and though this time he managed to stay closer to her on the stairs, outside he was no match for her. She ran swiftly into a wood and climbed a tree, where she hid until he gave up looking. When Cinderella's stepmother and stepsisters came home that night, they found her asleep as before, and did not think she heard them grumbling loudly about the maiden the prince had danced with once again for the entire evening.

On the third night of the ball, Cinderella again went to the hazel tree as soon as her stepmother and stepsisters had left, and said:

> Now hear my wish, my hazel tree:
> I need a dress to cover me.

This time the bird brought her the most beautiful dress in the world. It was neither gold nor silver, but it shimmered with a thousand muted colors, and had beautiful, shimmering slippers to match. The dress made all who saw it think of sunbeams dancing on the sea, and the shoes made them think of the delicate wings of dragonflies.

This time the prince had vowed he would not lose his lovely dancing partner. He had ordered his servants to coat the stairs to the ballroom with sticky pine pitch as soon as Cinderella arrived, and they did this promptly and thoroughly, while she was dancing with the prince as before. This time, when Cinderella ran down the stairs, she could not run quite so fast—and one of her slippers caught in the pitch and she had to leave it there or be caught.

The next morning the prince took the beautiful, shimmering slipper to his father the king and said, "My bride shall be the maiden whose foot fits this slipper—see how tiny and dainty it is! It belongs to the mysterious princess—for princess she must be—with whom I have danced the past three nights."

"Very well," said the king, "but now you must find her. Perhaps that will not be so easy. I wish you had danced with some of the other lovely maidens. But very well—go and look."

The prince set out that very day, and rode to the house of every person invited to the ball, and tried the slipper upon many a hopeful girl's foot—for they were all so anxious to be queen, they all pretended they had lost a slipper at the ball. But the lovely slipper fit no one; it was much too small for every maiden who tried it on.

At last the prince came to Cinderella's house, and said, "Surely the slipper belongs to someone who lives here, for I have been everywhere else."

The father was still not home, and the shrewd stepmother took her older daughter into her room to try the slipper on.

"Mother, it is too small," said the girl, struggling to squeeze into it. "Four toes will fit but not the fifth."

"Never mind," said the stepmother. "Just bend that toe under."

"I can hardly walk!" gasped the girl, when she had done so.

"No matter," said the stepmother. "When you are queen, you will have little need to walk. Just think of that, and all will be well." And she led her stepdaughter out to the prince, who took her hand and said, "Come with me, then, for the shoe is indeed on your foot." But, even though the girl managed to walk to the prince's coach without limping, the prince felt in his heart that something was not as it should be.

As the prince's coach passed by Cinderella's mother's grave, the birds of the forest flew around the coach and the silver gray bird lit on the prince's shoulder and said:

Good prince, you know not what you do:
Her toe is bent inside that shoe!

And so the prince bade the stepsister get down from the coach and walk with him awhile under the trees, saying that he wished to stretch his legs. By now the girl's toes had become so cramped she could barely walk, and when the prince touched the side of the slipper, he felt that one was bent under inside.

"You are not my true bride," he said angrily, and took her back to her parents' house.

"Surely it is my other daughter whom you want, then," said the stepmother calmly, and went with the younger girl into her bedroom.

"It does not fit, Mother," the girl said. "Almost—but I cannot get all my toes inside."

"Bend them under," said the stepmother as before, and she helped her second daughter squeeze her foot inside the slipper.

So once again the prince set off—but again he felt uneasy in his heart.

Soon they passed the hazel tree and the birds of the forest flew around the coach and the silver gray bird lit on the prince's shoulder and said:

> Good prince, you know not what you do:
> Her toes are bent inside that shoe!

And as before the prince bade the girl get out and walk with him, and she limped as her sister had limped, so he took her home again.

When he got there, the father had just returned from his journey and, having unhitched his horse, followed the prince and the second stepsister into the house. "Is there no other young girl in this house?" the prince was saying as the father came through the door. "For this is the last house to which invitations were sent."

"The maiden you want must not have been invited," said the stepmother, smooth as silk, "for there is no other girl here save my two daughters."

But at that the father looked from his wife to the prince and back again. "There is Cinderella," he said.

"Cinderella," said the prince. "And who might she be?"

"Oh," said the stepmother, glaring at her husband, "just a silly servant girl who scrubs and cleans and cooks in the kitchen. She is of no consequence."

At this Cinderella's father at last grew angry and he said, "She is my true daughter, wife, and of consequence to me!" And he sent for her.

This time the prince stood by while the slipper was tried on, and saw for himself that Cinderella's foot slid into it as easily as if it had been made for her. And this time he knew in his heart that he had found the right maiden. So he led her gently to his coach while her stepmother and stepsisters raged and her father rejoiced, and took her away with him to his palace. As they passed the hazel tree, the birds of the forest flew above them chirping merrily and the silver gray bird sang:

Good prince, you've found your bride so true:
See how her foot fits in the shoe!

"I have seen already," the prince said, smiling, and he did not make Cinderella get out and walk.

And very soon the king held another ball, in honor of the wedding of his son and his son's bride, and he invited Cinderella's father, but the stepmother and stepsisters had to sit at home by the fire and grumble, which is exactly what they continued doing for the rest of their days.

THE SIX SWANS

There was once a king who lived near a deep forest, and his greatest pleasure was to hunt.

One day he hunted a boar, who, instead of charging, ran from him, leading him deeper and deeper into the forest, and far from the servants and courtiers who accompanied him. It was not long before he lost sight of the boar altogether, and knew that he was lost. Every path he tried ended at a stump or a thicket or a stone, and none seemed to lead out into the open air.

Just as the sun began to set and he was about to despair, an old woman came toward him, wearing tattered black clothes and leaning on a gnarled stick. As she walked calmly, with no sign of fear, the king thought she must live near or in the forest, and would know the way out. So he went up to her and spoke. "Mistress," he said politely, "I see that you know your way in this wood; do you also know your way out of it? For I am lost, and must find my way home."

Now this woman was a witch and as such had her own use for the king. She had no intention of helping him without his paying a price for it.

"Sire," she said, twisting her head up to look at him, "I do know the way out, but before I tell you, you must promise to do something for me in return."

"And what is that?" asked the king, growing uneasy.

"Why, your majesty," said the witch, "it is well known that your good wife the queen died many years back, and left you with seven fine children to raise all alone, six fine boys and a girl as beautiful as the morning. Now I have a daughter myself, as lovely as any queen, and as she is a woman grown, she would make a fine mother for your children, and a good queen as well."

"But," said the king, "I have never seen your daughter, or spoken with her, and I am mourning still for my wife."

"You shall see my daughter when I lead you to her," replied the witch. "As for mourning your wife, that may be as it is, but think of your motherless children. You cannot be both father and mother at once to them."

"No," said the king, "I cannot. But if I am to marry again, I prefer to choose my own wife."

"Then," said the witch, "you may find your own way out of the forest." And she shuffled rapidly down the path, and vanished around a corner.

As soon as she had gone, the last of the setting sun slipped behind the distant hills, and the forest became dark and lonely. Wild beasts came out to hunt, and their eyes shone all around the king, who had no means of making a fire to scare them away. The same wild boar he had himself hunted earlier now seemed to be hunting him, for it came snuffling toward him—and at the very same moment the witch appeared again. "Now," she said shrewdly, "shall I take you to my daughter after all, and show you the way out?"

The king then understood that this part of the forest must be enchanted and that the boar and the other animals were in the witch's power. He knew he had no choice but to do as she said. So, with many fears, he consented.

The witch led him to a hovel among the trees, and by the fire stirring a pot of soup sat a young woman, lovely indeed, but not as lovely as the king's wife had been. She smiled at him, however, and spoke softly, and he began to think that marrying her might not be as unpleasant as he had thought. Nonetheless, as he went with her out of the forest, the witch pointing the way, uneasiness filled his heart again and he resolved to keep his children from his new wife no matter what it cost.

When he reached the palace, there was much rejoicing at his return. The king had his new queen shown to her chamber and then he sent for his children, the six fine boys and the girl as beautiful as the morning. Now this king had a number of castles, from which he defended the borders of his kingdom, and he told his children, pretending that it was an adventure, that he was sending them away that very night to live in one of them that was in a distant forest. "I will come often to see you," he told them. "Do not worry about that. And you will have the beasts and the birds for company, for all of the animals in that forest are tame, and every creature will be your friend." So saying, he embraced them all and entrusted them to the care of his oldest and wisest servant.

Now this castle was so well hidden that the king himself could not find it without aid, but he had a magic ball of twine that unrolled itself along the path to lead him there.

The next morning the king and the witch's daughter were married with great ceremony and afterward the new queen said, "Where are your children, husband? For I know from my mother that you have quite a number, and I saw none at our wedding."

"Oh," said the king, "did I not tell you? They have been living these many years with their grandmother, whose home is across the sea."

The witch's daughter did not believe him, but she kept silent, and watched carefully. Soon he began leaving the palace for long periods of time, saying he was hunting, and she grew suspicious. When she was sure he was not hunting at all but visiting his children, she bribed one of his weakest servants with gold, and at length discovered that her suspicion was correct. But the servant did not know where the king kept the magic ball of twine; he merely knew that the king used it for finding the distant castle. Every day thenceforth the witch's daughter hunted for the twine in vain, and every day also she sewed, making little shirts of white silk, six in all, for that is how many children she remembered her mother saying that the king had. Into each shirt with each stitch she sewed a charm known only to her.

One blustery day, when autumn had already stripped the trees bare of their leaves and the world was pulling in on itself in preparation for winter, the witch's daughter found the king's ball of twine stuffed into a corner of the darkest part of his stable. That very day, when the king went out to call on a neighboring duke, the witch's daughter took the ball of twine and the six silken shirts and the twine unrolled before her, showing her the way.

As she approached the castle in which the children, who were now nearly grown, were hidden, the six boys saw someone coming and, thinking it was their father, ran out to greet him. As the boys came running joyfully toward her, the witch's daughter threw the shirts into the air, and each one went straight to one of the king's sons, and covered him, changing him into a swan. The witch's daughter waited until she saw the six swans fly away over the treetops, and then returned to the palace, and put the ball of twine back in its place, well satisfied that she had gotten rid of the children and would now have the king all to herself.

On the next day, the king himself took his ball of twine and went to see his children, but he found his daughter weeping and no sign of his sons. "Where are your brothers?" the king asked.

"Oh, my father," said the girl, "they are gone! A woman came yesterday, and she had some shirts with her that she threw over my brothers and changed them to swans, and they flew away."

The king was greatly grieved to hear this. Afraid that his daughter would soon have the same evil fate, he said to her, "I will send all my soldiers and all my huntsmen out to look for your brothers, and they will soon be found. But you must come back with me to the palace, lest the same thing happen to you."

The girl pretended to agree, but asked her father if she could stay one more night in the forest castle. He at length agreed, and returned to the palace, saying he would come back the next day. But the girl had no intention of waiting until then, for she had a great dread of her stepmother, and feared that it was she who had enchanted her brothers. "I will leave here," she said to herself, "and walk in the direction my brothers took when they flew away, and perhaps I will find them myself."

So that very night, the king's daughter ran away. She walked steadily until the next afternoon, when she could walk no longer. Then she came upon a hut, and as it seemed empty, she went cautiously inside. There was a room with six beds in it, but she was afraid to lie in them, lest she be discovered, so she hid under the nearest one, and curled up to sleep. As the sun set, there was a whirring sound which grew rapidly in loudness and frightened the girl so that she woke and huddled in fear.

In a moment a great bird flew in an open window and settled on one of the beds, and it was a swan. Then another bird came, and a third and a fourth, till there were six in all, and they turned to one another and flapped their wings, making a great wind, and lo, their feathers and swan skins fell to the ground like garments and the girl saw her very own brothers again. Then she came out from under the bed with a cry of joy, and embraced her brothers and wept with them and they with her.

"I will stay here," she said to them, "and we will all be safe from the terrible witch who did this to you."

"Alas, no, sister," they told her. "You cannot stay here, for this house belongs to robbers, not to us, and they will kill you if they find you here. We ourselves only use it when they are gone."

"Why, then we will leave here," said the girl, "and find a house of our own, or build one."

"Alas, sister," the brothers said, "we cannot do that. For we can be human only for one quarter of an hour each evening, right at sunset, and that time is almost up for this evening. In a minute we will be swans again, and can do nothing but fly and float on the water; we cannot build houses or live in them."

"Is there nothing that can be done?" asked the girl. "If you can be human for fifteen minutes a day there must be some way that will allow you to be human forever."

"Alas," they told her, "there is a way, but it is so hard you cannot do it."

"I?" said the girl in surprise. "Is it I, then, who can free you?"

"Only you," said the brothers sadly, "but to free us you must remain silent for six years, without speaking or laughing, and you must gather wild lavender asters, and spin their petals into yarn, and weave cloth of it, and from the cloth make six shirts. And if you say so much as 'Good day' to anyone, or let one tiny laugh pass your lips in all that time, the aster petals will wither, and whatever you have made of them—yarn or cloth or shirts—will fall away into dust."

The girl set her lips firmly and stood tall and straight and said, "Then these are the last words I shall speak for six long years: I will free you, my brothers." Before she had finished, the fifteen minutes were up, and the six young men before her turned back into swans and had to fly away.

Nevertheless, the girl was determined. She left the robbers' hut and found herself a tree with wide, sheltering branches. There she settled herself and slept. And the next morning she was up with the sun, searching for lavender asters. Not far from her tree she found a great meadow, and as the cruel frost had not yet touched it, it was carpeted with the lovely flowers, which look like daisies except that where daisies have white petals, they have reddish blue ones, of softest lavender.

All day the king's daughter gathered asters and took them back to her tree nest. And all the next day she did the same, and the next as well. On the third day, the king of the next land, which was not far from the edge of this forest, came a-hunting, and his huntsmen found her. "Good day," they said politely, stooping down to smile at her where she sat with her asters under the tree.

But she only nodded without speaking, and returned to her work. She was now separating the petals from the flowers and putting them carefully in a pile.

"We will not hurt you," one of the king's huntsmen said. "Only come out to us and you will see."

But she shook her head and continued working.

At last the king himself rode up, and he was so struck by the girl's beauty that he went under the tree, and in every language he knew, which was a great many, he said, "Who are you and how came you here?" But she remained mute as before.

"Well," said the king to his men, "we cannot leave her here; she will perish when the cold comes." So he held out his hand to the girl and beckoned, but she would not come. So at last he had his huntsmen seize her, but she fought and kicked and scratched—although in silence—and pointed to her piles of flowers and of petals, until the king said, "Stop! I think she will not go without those flowers; see what she does if you pick them up—carefully, for she was taking great pains with them."

So the huntsmen put the petals and the remaining whole asters gently into the large sacks they had for carrying game, and the girl stood quietly by, nodding and smiling to let them know they were doing what she wished. And so at last the king was able to lift her to his horse, and she rode with him peacefully to his palace, every once in a while looking back to make sure she still had her flowers with her.

When they reached the palace, the king gave the girl rich clothes and costly jewels and allowed her to dress like a princess—and of course she was one in her own country, but he did not know that. When she smiled he saw that she was as beautiful as the morning, but still she would not speak. Even so, as the days passed and the girl quietly worked with her flowers, now spinning the petals into a soft lavender yarn, the king grew to love her. At length, he asked her to be his wife.

The girl saw no reason not to marry him, for he was kind and good and in all ways treated her gently, and she had grown to love him also. It saddened her greatly that she could not speak to him, but it pleased her that he never kept her from her work. From time to time he had even helped her with it by having more asters gathered for her when she needed them; in the spring, he had told her, he would plant some in the palace garden. And so she agreed to marry him and the wedding was accomplished.

All in the palace rejoiced save one—the king's mother, who was jealous of the young girl, and suspicious of her. "For," she said to herself, "who can tell what manner of creature she is since she does not speak and spends all her time making yarn out of flower petals? Since she is like no other person, she must be a witch!"

The next year, when half the lavender yarn was spun and the palace looms were dressed with it, ready for weaving, the young queen gave birth to a fine baby—but the king's mother took it from her as she slept and hid it, and put blood on the queen's hands and on her gown. And then she went to her son, pretending to be sad and said, "Alas, your wife has killed her own child, come and see!" And the king went to his wife, and saw her staring in shock at her own hands, which were covered in blood, as were her garments. And she was so shocked that she would not even nod or shake her head when the king questioned her. "See," said the king's mother, "she must be guilty, for she will not even defend herself!"

But the king did not believe his gentle wife would do such a terrible deed, and so he loved and protected her as before, and grieved with her over the baby. Two years passed, three since the queen had seen her brothers in the robbers' hut. By now she had spun enough yarn for all the shirts and woven half enough cloth. And once again she gave birth to a lovely child, but the king's mother took it away, hiding it and putting blood on the queen's hands and on her gown as before. "Alas," she said to the king, "your wife is truly evil; she is some kind of monster to kill her own child." But again the king, although a tiny doubt began to creep into his mind, did not believe her. If only my wife could speak, he thought, I am sure she could tell me the truth. Nonetheless, he tried to go on as before, and was almost as loving as ever toward his wife.

In two and a half more years, when the cloth was all woven and the shirts cut out and some of them already stitched, the queen gave birth to a child and the king's mother took it away while she was sleeping. And this time the king was not so patient and trusting. "You must tell me!" he thundered at his wife. "You must at least nod your head or shake it. Did you kill your child?"

But the young queen, who had tried to stay awake to see who it was who took her child, was so exhausted and so grieved that once more she could only stare at her hands.

So the king, though it saddened him, had her thrown into the palace dungeon, hoping that she would come to her senses there and let him know the truth. Because six years were now nearly up, the queen worked feverishly to finish the shirts—for the king had at least allowed her to have her cloth and her needles and thread and scissors in her dungeon cell.

When it was clear she was not going to speak or answer the king's questions by any sign, the king's advisers told him he must put her on trial, for there was grumbling in the kingdom about her, and rumors that she was a witch. So the king, again with sadness, agreed, and the young queen was brought to court and questioned—but she was afraid that nodding or shaking would lead to speaking, and so she sat silently sewing, and if anyone tried to take her sewing from her, she wept and fought vigorously.

"There is nothing to do, your majesty," said the judges, "but to put her to death; the people demand it, and, indeed, she does appear to be a witch. Look at her, the way she endlessly stitches those shirts! Surely there is some evil there; best she be destroyed and the shirts with her."

And when the feeling against the queen grew so strong that the people threatened to rise up against the king, he had to give in.

The terrible day dawned, and the sky was dark and ominous when the young queen was led to where the fire had been prepared for her—for burning was the punishment in those days for witches. On her arm she carried the six lavender shirts and they were all completed save for the left sleeve of the last one. All the crowd cheered to see that the shirts were going to the fire with her; because they did not understand what they were, they were sure they were instruments of evil.

Just as the young queen was taken to the fire, there was a whirring sound and a sudden brightness against the sky, and six swans flew down and surrounded her. She rejoiced, for she knew her brothers had returned. She threw a shirt over each, and lo, they turned to men again—all save the sixth, whose right arm became human, but whose left remained a wing. The brothers embraced their sister and led her away from the fire. She then went to her husband and said, "At last I can speak to you," and she told him all that had happened, from the beginning. So the king's mother had to tell where she had hidden the three babies, and after they had been found, she was punished. Then the young queen's father was sent for and reunited with his seven children. As his wife, the witch's daughter, was now dead, they all passed the remainder of their days in peace and joy.

THE GIRL WITHOUT HANDS

A MILLER can only prosper when farmers bring him grain to grind, and when there is no grain, he has nothing. Now once upon a time there was a miller to whom this happened. One summer when the weather was dry, the grain withered in the fields, so no one brought him any to grind, and he became as poor as the farmers whose crops had failed. Soon he had nothing left but his house, his mill, and the fine, old apple tree behind it.

The miller was not the kind of person who gave up easily, however, and he decided to try to make ends meet by cutting wood and selling it. He went into the forest with his axe and had not been chopping long before an old man whom he had never seen stepped from behind a tree. "What a terrible job woodcutting is," the old man said, clucking his tongue—but his eyes held an evil glint. "I do not see why anyone does it."

"Nor do I," said the miller, leaning upon his axe for a moment's rest, "but I have no choice, as there is no grain for me to grind in my mill."

"A miller, are you?" said the old man, laying his arm across the miller's shoulders. "Well, well. Tell you what, friend miller, I will make you as rich as you like, if you will promise to give me that which is standing behind your mill."

Well, thought the miller, the old apple tree is the only thing that stands behind my mill. He may certainly have that if he can make me rich! And so aloud he said, "I will promise you that, stranger, if you will indeed make me rich."

"Good, good," said the old man, and, leading the miller to the stump of a tree he had just cut, he wrote out two copies of the agreement they had just made.

The moment the miller and the old man had each signed both copies of the agreement, the old man began to laugh.

"Something amuses you," said the miller. "What? It is a solemn agreement we have just made!"

"It is, it is," said the old man—but he still laughed, and his eyes still showed their evil gleam. "Well, well—you must go home now and enjoy your riches. I will return in three years' time and take what you have promised to give me." Laughing still, the old man left.

The miller did not like the sound of the old man's laughter, but he did like the idea of being rich and, as he had his copy of the agreement in his pocket, he was sure the old man would have to fulfill his promise. And sure enough, when the miller walked up to his house, his wife ran out to meet him, crying, "Husband, husband, you cannot imagine what has happened! Just look!" She led him inside, and he saw that every box, every chest, every cupboard and drawer was filled with gold. "I do not understand how this can be," said the wife, laughing as she let a shower of gold coins fall through her fingers, "but one minute all was as it has been since we became poor, and the next, every container was filled to bursting with gold."

"I know how it happened," said the miller, and he told his wife about the old man he had met in the forest. "And so," he finished, "I, of course, promised to give him what stands behind the mill—for with all this gold, we can surely afford to give up the apple tree. He will not even be coming for it until three years have passed, so we will have apples for some time to come."

But much to the miller's astonishment, his wife threw her apron over her face and began to wail. "Oh, husband, husband!" she cried. "Oh, how can you have done such a terrible thing?"

"What terrible thing have I done?" asked the miller angrily. "Is bringing us wealth a terrible thing?"

"Bringing it by this means is a terrible thing," said the wife, "for only the Devil makes such bargains. Today not only did the apple tree stand behind the mill but also our daughter, who was sweeping the mill yard at the very hour you were in the forest."

Now the miller himself was distraught, but he tried to comfort his wife and himself by saying that perhaps the Devil had meant the tree after all. "For how could he have known our child stood there?" he said.

"The Evil One," answered his wife, "knows everything he wishes to know, and sees everything he wishes to see."

"But," said the miller, "perhaps it was not the Devil after all."

And they discussed it for the next three years as they went mournfully about their business, getting scant enjoyment from their wealth.

Now the miller's daughter was beautiful and good and pious and in the three years that soon passed she never did a single wrong. On the day the Devil was to return, she washed herself spotlessly clean and drew a circle around herself with chalk, for she had heard that both these actions would protect her.

The Devil appeared at the very same hour he had come three years before, and reached out to take the girl, but then drew back, for he found he could not go near her. "Miller," he said, so angrily his eyes flashed fire, "take the chalk away from this girl, and do not let her have more water. Do not let her wash, for when she has done so, I may not approach her. Heed me, miller, and do as I say! You must keep your bargain with me, or greater ills than you can imagine will fall upon you and all your family."

The miller was so terrified that he obeyed, and the next morning the Devil came again. But the girl had spent all night weeping, resting her face upon her hands, and so her hands once more were spotlessly clean. When he saw this, the Devil was so angry his voice crackled as he spoke. "Miller," he bellowed, "you must cut her hands off, for she has wept on them and they are too clean!"

"I cannot do that," cried the miller in great alarm. "How could I cut off my own child's hands?"

"It is as you wish," snarled the Devil, "but if you do not, such disasters as you cannot imagine will befall not only you and yours but the entire kingdom as well." As the Devil spoke, the wind rose and the sky darkened, and forked lightning split a nearby tree in two.

"Father," said the girl, when the Devil had gone away, "you must do as he says."

"My child, I cannot," wept the miller. "Truly, I cannot hurt you."

"I shall pray," said the girl, "and God will protect me. Father, you must do as he says—see how the sky darkens still! The wind is trying to tear the roof off the mill, and soon it will reach the village and destroy the church and all the houses." Kneeling, the girl held out her hands and said, "Do what you must do, Father"—and so the miller did.

But that night the girl wept upon the stumps of her arms, and the next day when the Devil came for her, he again could not go near her. Since this was the third time, he lost his right to claim her, and had to go away without her.

"Oh, my poor child," said the miller. "It is through you that I have received my wealth, for it is you the Devil wanted in exchange. No father has ever had a more loving, obedient child. I promise that I will keep you handsomely for your whole life long; you will want for nothing. All my wealth will go to you."

"No, Father," said the girl gently. "I would not be a burden to you. I shall go forth into the world and make my own way."

The miller and his wife both begged their daughter to stay, but she insisted that she be allowed to go, and in the end they had to give in. She asked them to bind her arms close to her body, and left that very day.

At nightfall she came to the king's garden, which was surrounded by a broad moat. In the moonlight she could see pear trees heavy with fruit, and as she had not eaten all day, her mouth watered and she felt near fainting from hunger. "Oh, that I might be able to go into that garden and eat of that fruit—but I cannot cross the moat, and so must be content," she said to herself. Then she knelt down outside the garden and prayed for strength.

Suddenly an angel came to her, dressed in shimmering robes. The angel smiled and lifted her to her feet, and dammed up the water of the moat so that a path appeared for the girl without hands to walk on. The angel led her across the moat and into the garden. The grateful girl reached up to a low branch by tilting her head and just managed to grasp one pear in her teeth and eat it. After that, her hunger eased, so she crawled into the bushes to sleep.

Now the king's gardener was keeping watch nearby, but when he saw the angel he dared not speak or show himself, though he knew the king counted all his fruit every morning, and would soon miss the pear. And it fell out as the gardener expected. In the morning, when the dew was still moist on the grass, the king came into the garden, counted the pears, and found one missing. "It does not seem to be lying beneath the tree," said the king to his gardener, "so it cannot have fallen. Do you know where it is?"

"Sire," said the gardener, "last night a spirit with no hands came into your garden. It reached up with its mouth and ate one of your pears."

"But the moat!" said the king. "How did the spirit cross the moat? Did it have wings?"

"No, sire," said the gardener. "It did not even have hands, as I have told you. But with it was a being in shimmering robes who parted the water and led the spirit across."

"And why," asked the king, "did you not stop the spirit when you saw what it was about to do?"

"Sire," said the gardener, "I know of nothing save angels who can part water, and so I was afraid and did not move."

"Well," said the king, frowning, "I will watch with you tonight, and we will see if the same thing happens again."

So that night the king stayed in the garden, and before long the girl without hands came out of the bushes and reached up with her mouth for another pear.

The king stood still till she had eaten, for he found himself moved to pity by her beauty and by the trouble she had to put herself to in order to reach the pear. Then he showed himself and asked, "Lovely creature, have you come here from heaven? Or are you of this earth? Are you a spirit as my gardener thinks, or are you a mortal person?"

"I am from this earth," the girl without hands replied modestly, "and am the saddest of mortals, for all save God have deserted me."

"I do not understand how anyone could desert such a one as you," the king replied. "*I* would never do so." He placed his royal hand upon her shoulder. "Come," he said, "for you must be hungry for more than pears. Come—I have not yet dined; you will be company for me."

The girl let herself be guided into the palace, where the king sat with her at his finely appointed table; they dined deliciously upon pheasants and jellies, salads, cakes, and cream. The poor miller's daughter had never seen such fare, and the king fed every morsel to her with his own hands. Later, he ordered his musicians to sing and play for her softly until she fell asleep.

It was not long before the king came to love the girl without hands, and she him. On the day he married her, he gave her a pair of silver hands for a wedding present, and the two lived happily together for the next twelvemonth.

After a year, however, when the young queen was expecting her first child, the king had to go away with his army for he knew not how long. The day before he left, he went to his mother, who lived in the palace with them, and said, "Mother, please watch over my wife as if she were your own daughter. And should our child arrive before I return, care for mother and baby well, and inform me at once in a letter of how they are."

Not long after the king left, his wife gave birth to a fine baby boy, and the king's mother quickly wrote him the joyful news and entrusted the letter to a messenger. But the king was far away by then, and the messenger had to rest halfway through his journey. While he lay sleeping beside a brook, the Devil came by. "Oho," cried Old Scratch, "I shall now get even with the faithless miller and his ever-so-pious daughter." And he sat quickly down on a stump and wrote a false letter saying that the young queen had given birth to a monster, not a child at all. Then he took the letter the king's mother had written, and put in its place his own false one.

When the king read the false letter he was sorely troubled, but out of his great love he wrote gently to his mother, telling her to take great care of his wife till he could come home again—which, alas, was not to be for some time—and to care for the monster as well, for it was his own and he would love it. Back the messenger went, but he rested again beside the same brook, and the Devil once more came to him and substituted his own harsh letter for the good king's gentle one; his letter ordered that the queen and her child be put to death.

When the king's mother read this letter she was shocked beyond belief. "My son would never say such a thing," she said to herself. "There must be error here; I will write again." And so she did, many times over, and each time the Devil exchanged the real letter for one of his own, and in the last one he ordered that the mother and child be killed without further delay, and that the queen's tongue be sent to him as proof that the deed had been done.

Again the king's mother could not believe what she read, but this time the words of the letter were so harsh that she felt she must at least appear to obey. She commanded the royal hunters to get her the tongue of a hind, which they did, and then she said to the young queen, "I dare not have you stay here, for there is clearly great mischief afoot. You must, alas, go out into the wide world, you and the little one, and I pray that all will be well with you." The old mother helped the queen tie her child upon her back, and the queen left the palace weeping, sure that her husband was angry with her.

When she came to the shelter of a forest, she fell exhausted to her knees and commenced to pray. And the angel with the shimmering robes came again to her and said, "Follow me, and do not fear," and led her to a little house deep within the forest. Over the door of the house was a sign that said: "Here everyone is free."

The angel went away again, but a maiden in a snow white dress came to the door and, curtsying, said, "Welcome, Lady Queen," and led her inside. She helped the young queen untie the child and feed him, and then laid him down in a little cradle, soft and warm.

"But how did you know I am a queen?" asked the mother softly, when the child was asleep and they were rocking him.

The maiden smiled and said, "I, too, am an angel, sent to watch over you and the little one—for you are a good woman, and have been much wronged."

For seven years the queen and her child lived in the forest with the angel, and each year, the good queen's hands grew back a little more, till they were whole again.

At long last, weary and lonely, the king was able to come home from the wars and before he even rested or ate he wished to see his wife and son. "He must be quite a lad now, eh?" he said to his old mother, full of hope that she would say the child was not a monster at all. "Does he shoot yet with a bow and arrow? Does he ride the royal ponies?" He laughed then and said, "I know, I know—you will tell me that he has barely learned to walk and talk. But that is fine—for then I myself will teach him to shoot and to ride."

The old mother wept at his words and cried, "My son, how can you be so cruel! Did you not write and ask me to kill both your wife and her child; and to save the queen's tongue as proof? Here it is." She showed him the hind's tongue that she had so carefully and fearfully preserved, and watched his face closely.

The king stared and stared at the tongue and after a long moment he said, "Alas, mother, I asked no such deed of you, nor would I ever. How is it that you believed such a lie and how is it that you yourself were so cruel as to carry out such a wicked deed?" But he spoke sadly rather than with anger.

"Oh, my son," said the mother, falling to her knees before him, "I did not do the deed, and I am overjoyed that you did not ask it. The tongue is a hind's tongue, and I merely sent your wife and child away from here."

"And the child?" asked the king. "The child was—well? The child was as other children are?"

"Why, yes," said the mother, and then the king told her about the letters he had received, and she told him about hers. "I feared the wars had harmed your reason," said the mother, "and so I did send your wife and child away for their own safety as well as for mine. The dear queen believed you were angry with her and she went forth weeping, with your son tied upon her back."

Then the king lamented mightily, but in a while, when he had recovered himself, he said, "I will go forth and seek her. I will go as far as the blue sky, and I will not eat nor shall I drink until I have found my wife and my poor son."

And so the king went forth, and, indeed, he was too distraught with grief and longing to think of food or drink as he sought his family in every forest cave and upon every mountain, and beside the great salt sea. For seven long years he journeyed, and though he neither ate nor drank, God did not allow him to die.

At the end of the seventh year, the king came into the forest in which lived his wife and son, and found the little house with the sign saying: "Here everyone is free." And the maiden in white came to the door saying, "Welcome, Lord King," and led him inside. "Where have you come from?" she asked gently, when she had showed him a seat by the fire.

"From far," said the king. "I have traveled these seven years seeking my wife and child."

The angel smiled wisely, but did not speak further except to offer the king food—but he refused, saying he wished only to sleep. So she showed him to a bed, and he lay gratefully upon it, spreading his handkerchief over his face, for the sun streamed in through the open window.

And now the angel went quickly into another room where the queen was with her son, whom the queen called Sorrowful, and said, "Lady Queen, your patience has been rewarded; your husband the king is here, asleep in the next room."

The queen leaped to her feet, her hand to her throat, and her heart fluttered wildly with joy. "Sorrowful, come," she said, and ran into the other room.

When they entered, a breeze blew the handkerchief from the king's face, and the queen, seeing that the sun shone on his closed eyes, said, "Sorrowful, pick up your father's handkerchief and cover his face lest he wake before he is rested."

So Sorrowful picked up the handkerchief and carefully placed it again over the king's eyes.

Now even in his sleep the king heard his wife's voice, and it gave him great joy, though he had been so long away he was not certain that it was she. Even so, he twitched his nose to make the handkerchief fall again.

"Sorrowful," said the queen, "please pick up your father's handkerchief once more."

"Mother," said Sorrowful, "I will, but why do you call this man my father? You have taught me that I have no father in this world, but only my Father in heaven, to whom I pray. Therefore this man cannot be my father."

At that the king could contain himself no longer; he sat up—but the queen, still fearing his anger, turned away so that he could not see her face. "Good morrow, lady," said the king, as calmly as he could, "and who are you, and this beautiful child?"

"Oh, sir," said the queen, her head bent low, "I am the queen your wife, and this is Sorrowful, your princely son."

The king was sure in his heart that this was so, but he saw the queen's hands and said gently, "Ah, but my wife had silver hands, not hands of flesh."

The queen, weeping now as the king's mother had wept, answered, "Sir, you made me hands of silver for our wedding, in the days when you truly loved me and did not wish to cast me out. In the years that I have been here, God has allowed my human hands to grow again, and so you see me as I am."

Then the curtains in the doorway stirred and the angel came in, bearing the silver hands, and she showed them to the king. And the king, seeing at last that the woman before him was his own dear wife, took the queen in his arms and begged her forgiveness. She embraced him and said, "Oh, my husband, I do forgive you—for I do believe it was the Devil who wrote those terrible letters!"

"The heaviest of stones has fallen from my heart," the king replied, and then he smiled and went down upon one knee and patted the other, saying, "Now Sorrowful, come here and sit on my knee—for you have two fathers now; the one in heaven and this one, who is on earth and will teach you to ride a pony and shoot a bow and arrow. And who," he said, looking up at his wife once more, "thinks we should call our son Joyful from this day forth."

And so they did. On that same day, the king broke his seven-year fast and the angel in white and the king and queen and young Joyful dined on all manner of dainties. And then the king and his family journeyed back to the palace, where they rejoiced with the king's mother and then settled down to live in peace for many years to come.

FITCHER'S BIRD

Now this is a story for those who are not squeamish, for it is about a wicked wizard who liked to cut people up.

This wicked wizard's name was Fitcher, and he used to go about disguised as a poor man, with a basket into which he put his victims and carried them away. His power was such that all he had to do was touch someone, and that person could not move away from him and had to do what he wanted.

One day Fitcher, disguised as a poor beggar, went to the house of a man who he knew had three lovely daughters and as many sons. He had his basket with him. "Alms, alms for the poor," he cried weakly, approaching the man's door. Out came the oldest daughter with a piece of bread. When Fitcher reached for it, he touched the maiden's hand, and she was then in his power and had to get into the basket and be carried off.

He took her to his house, which was very rich and beautiful, and which stood in the middle of a dark and dismal forest. All around were strange beasts and birds that Fitcher had enchanted.

At first, Fitcher treated the maiden kindly and gave her everything she wanted. But that did not last long. Within a few days he said, "My dear, I must go on a journey, but you will be quite safe. Here are the keys to the house, which you are free to explore all you like; I think you will find much that pleases you. But you may not go into the room that the smallest key opens." He handed her the keys and pointed out the smallest one. Then he gave her an egg, saying, "Take this egg with you wherever you go, and be very careful with it, for if it is lost, great misfortune will follow."

The maiden was curious, but she promised to obey Fitcher in everything he said. As soon as he was gone she began exploring, and she found many wondrous things—rooms with rich furnishings, silver and gold in great chests, strange birds with sweeping feathers, bottles and jars of magic potions—but these were in a locked cabinet for which there was no key. Several times she passed by the door of the forbidden room, but at last she could no longer stifle her curiosity, so she unlocked the door.

As soon as she was inside, she gasped and wished that she had not gone in, for in the center of the room stood a large cauldron filled with blood and the remains of cut-up people. The maiden was so frightened at the sight that she dropped the egg into the cauldron. Quickly she pulled it out and, glad to see that it was still whole, she wiped the blood off—but the blood appeared again immediately, and no matter how she washed it, she could not get the egg to stay clean.

When Fitcher came back, he greeted the maiden and said, "Now where are my keys and where is the egg?"

"Here they are," she said, handing him the keys first and then, trembling, the egg.

When he saw the stains on the egg, he knew she had disobeyed him. He seized her, killed her, and added her body to those in the cauldron.

Then he set off for the same house again.

"Alms, alms for the poor!" he cried in a piteous voice, and soon the second daughter came out with a piece of bread. He touched her as he had touched her sister, and she had to get into the basket and let him carry her to his house in the woods. All happened as before, and soon Fitcher went off again with his basket, this time to fetch the third and youngest sister.

The youngest sister was also the cleverest, and she was already suspicious of Fitcher. Again, all happened as before: Fitcher carried the youngest sister away in his basket, treated her kindly at first, and then, in a few days, told her he must go on a journey. He gave her the keys and the egg, and instructed her as he had instructed her sisters.

But this maiden first put the egg away in a box lined with goosedown. Then with great care she explored the house, and came at last to the room she was not to enter. Like her sisters, she went in, but she kept her wits about her—though she cried out and then wept when she saw what was in the cauldron. But soon she dried her eyes and with determination she set about gathering the parts of her sisters together. Soon she had laid all the pieces out correctly—and lo! when she had done so, her sisters' arms and legs began to grow together with their bodies and soon they could move and speak and were in all ways whole. The three maidens then likewise helped the other poor victims in the cauldron, who thanked them joyfully many times over and then hastened away to their homes.

But the sisters whispered together, making plans. When all was decided, the youngest hid the other two in a little room Fitcher rarely entered. Then she waited for him to come home.

When Fitcher arrived, he greeted the youngest sister and demanded, "Where are my keys and my egg?" She brought him both, and the egg was white and unstained.

"My dear," he said after he had examined it, "you have passed the test all others have failed; you shall be my bride."

The maiden was not pleased with that, but she pretended that she was, and agreed. And that meant that Fitcher could no longer have power over her, and that he had to do everything she wished.

"Before I can marry you," she said, "you must share your gold with my poor mother and father; I shall put some in a basket for you and you must carry it to them on your back. While you are gone I will get ready."

Fitcher was not pleased with that, but he knew he had to agree.

The maiden, saying she would fill the basket, went to where she had hidden her sisters and said, "Rejoice, for we can now fulfill our plan. Climb into this basket, and he will carry you home—but remember, as soon as you arrive, send our father and brothers and all our cousins to help."

The older girls climbed into the basket, and their youngest sister then covered them carefully with gold. Then she called Fitcher and, showing him the basket, said, "You must now carry this to my father's house—but do not stop along the way, not even to rest. I shall be watching you through my little window and if you stop I will know."

The wizard lifted the basket onto his back, and carried it away, but it was heavy, and sweat poured off his face with the effort of carrying it. After a while he felt he could go no further, so he sat down. But before he had eased the basket from his shoulders, the oldest sister cried, "What, Fitcher, did I not tell you not to rest? I can see you through my little window; go on your way!"

Fitcher thought it was his bride-to-be who spoke, and, as he had to do whatever she wished, he stood up again and walked on.

Again he grew tired and, thinking now he must surely be so far away she could no longer see him, he sat down again. Just as he was about to untie the basket, the second sister cried, "Fitcher, you lazy creature, I see you from my little window! Get up and go on!"

So up Fitcher got, and every time he wanted to rest, one or the other sister ordered him on. So in a while, exhausted, he stumbled into the parents' house, and dropped the basket on the floor. Then, gasping, he sank down to rest—and while his back was turned, the two girls crept out of the basket and spoke to their father and brothers and sent for their cousins.

Meanwhile, the youngest sister saw to it that Fitcher's house was made clean for the wedding, and she sent invitations to all the friends whose names were listed in a book of his she found. Then she took a skull that he, being a wizard, used as an ornament, and decked it with flowers and jewels so that from a distance, it would look like a living person.

When the day came for the wedding guests to arrive, the bride-to-be poured honey all over herself, and then she cut open a feather bed and rolled in the feathers until she looked like a feathered creature herself—like one of Fitcher's strange birds. Then she hopped down the path leading from the house, bobbing her head and holding her arms like wings. Soon she met a party of wedding guests, who, since they were the wizard's

friends, were used to seeing strange creatures around him. "Look at the great bird," they said to each other. "It must be one of Fitcher's creatures." One guest went up to the feathered-covered maiden and said, "Good day, Fitcher's bird. Where have you come from?"

"I have come from Fitcher's house," said the maiden.

"Ah," said the guest, "then you must know what the bride is doing?"

"Yes, indeed," said the maiden. "She has cleaned the house from top to bottom, and made all ready for the wedding. Now she is watching from her window for the bridegroom to return."

The guests went on, and in time the maiden met Fitcher himself.

Now Fitcher had so many strange creatures around him that he did not remember them all, but he knew he might easily have a bird such as this one, and so he said, "Good day, Fitcher's bird—for you must have come from my house, did you not?"

"Yes," said the maiden, taking great care to disguise her voice.

"Ah," said the wizard, "then can you tell me what my bride is doing?"

"I can," said the maiden. "She has made all ready for the wedding and she is now watching from the window for your return."

So Fitcher walked on toward his house, and the maiden walked on toward her father's house. Fitcher reached his destination first—but on her way the maiden met her father and brothers and cousins.

When Fitcher drew closer to his house, he looked up to the little window and saw from a distance the decorated skull. Thinking it was his bride, he waved and smiled and called out to her. Then he hurried the rest of the way and in time reached the house and went inside.

While he was preparing himself for his wedding, changing his travel-stained clothes, the maiden's father and brothers and cousins arrived. They sent the wedding guests away, and locked the doors of the house and burned it down with Fitcher in it, and so he troubled no one ever again. The three sisters lived on with their parents and, in time, all married happily and lived in joy with their husbands.